JAMESTOWN  PUBLISHERS

# FRIGHT WRITE

# Deadly Detours

# FRIGHT WRITE

## A FRIGHTENINGLY FUN Reading and Writing Program

# Deadly Detours

## Write Your Own Disastrous Travel Tale

JAMESTOWN PUBLISHERS

*a division of* NTC/CONTEMPORARY PUBLISHING GROUP
Lincolnwood, Illinois USA

*Editorial Director:* Cynthia Krejcsi

*Executive Editor:* Marilyn Cunningham

*Editorial Services Manager:* Sylvia Bace

*Market Development Manager:* Mary Sue Dillingofski

*Design Manager:* Ophelia M. Chambliss

*Production and Design:* PiperStudiosInc

*Cover Composition:* Doug Besser

*Production Manager:* Margo Goia

ISBN: 0-89061-861-5

Published by Jamestown Publishers,

a division of NTC/Contemporary Publishing Group, Inc.,

4255 West Touhy Avenue,

Lincolnwood (Chicago), Illinois 60646-1975 U.S.A.

# Contents

## To the Reader

# WARNING!

The stories in this book could give you nightmares. With any luck, these stories will also make your hair stand on end, give you goose bumps, and send chills up your spine. They'll probably make you think twice before going on your next vacation, too.

But if you pay close attention, these stories can also help you become a frightfully good writer. See how professional writers grab your attention and build suspense. Find out how to write convincing dialogue and weave haunting details throughout a story. Learn how to write stories that will make your teacher's flesh crawl.

Learn how to **FrightWrite!**

# Solo Flight

## Have you ever looked forward to a trip for weeks, only to have it turn into a real nightmare?

Ever dream that you're flying like a superhero? That's what riding in a sailplane feels like. It's just you and the wind, soaring through the sky free and easy like some huge, magnificent eagle. It's a <u>sensation</u> most kids can only dream about.

I'm one of the lucky ones. My dad has taken me up in sailplanes since I was old enough to wear a crash helmet. I've probably <u>logged</u> more hours in the air than most kids have logged on their bicycles. If I could, I'd spend my whole life riding the air currents . . . and I almost did.

It was the end of June. The big Fourth of July weekend was coming up, and it was also going to be my twelfth birthday. Mom and Dad had a special present in store for me. They were going to let me take my first solo flight. Although I'd flown our sailplane countless times with Dad in the cockpit, this would be the first time I'd be going up all by myself.

"Are you sure I'm old enough?" I asked anxiously when they told me of their plans.

**sensation:** a strong or excited feeling

**logged:** recorded the number of flights

"It's not a question of age, Keisha, but experience," my father replied calmly. "Anyone can fly a sailplane if they have the right training. Personally, I'd rather have *you* at the controls than half the adult pilots I know!"

"You'll do fine, Keisha," my mother assured me. Mom was quite a glider pilot herself. In fact, my parents met while soaring past each other at five thousand feet! "Of course, if you don't want to . . ."

"No, I do!" I quickly cut in. "It's just that this kind of caught me by surprise, that's all."

"I remember the first time I soloed," my dad said, his eyes suddenly taking on that weird, faraway look parents have when they start talking about the past. "I wasn't much older than you. It made me feel stronger and freer than I ever had in my life. It's a feeling you're not going to forget for as long as you live."

As it turned out, my dad was absolutely right.

❊ ❊ ❊

"Ready to go, Keisha?" my mother called from the foot of the stairs.

"In a second!" I yelled back. I was in my bedroom getting myself prepared both physically and mentally for my big day. I'd already spent an entire hour putting together my wardrobe, and now I was standing in front of the full-length mirror on my bedroom door, checking myself out. I was wearing my lucky green shirt, my lucky jeans with the holes in the knees, my lucky leather belt with the silver belt buckle, my lucky red socks I'd worn when I pitched my one and only no-hitter, and, of course,

**PREDICT**

*Do you think this flight will be as perfect as Keisha thinks it will be?*

my lucky running shoes with barely any tread left on them. There was only one thing missing.

Going over to my dresser, I opened the small jewelry box on top of it. Inside, nestled among the various pins, commemorative coins, and other assorted odds and ends I'd collected over the years, was a set of silver pilot's wings. They had belonged to my grandfather—my dad's dad— who died before I was even born. My grandfather had been an Air Force fighter pilot during the Vietnam War. In 1966, at the age of thirty-five, he was shot down and killed by a North Vietnamese antiaircraft missile. My dad, who was only ten years old at the time, was given these wings at his father's funeral. For some reason, the wings had not been pinned to his dad's uniform when he was buried. My father never wore these wings himself, but thought I might want to when I became a real pilot. This seemed like the perfect time.

I lifted the small metal wings from the box and carefully pinned them to my left breast pocket. Then I checked myself out again in the mirror. The wings hung straight and true, just like I'm sure my grandfather had always flown. I gave myself a crisp salute, then turned and headed out the door.

"So what are we waiting for?" I shouted as I thundered down the stairs. "Let's fly!"

Our sailplane was <u>hangared</u> at the Sky Harbor Airport, which is about fifteen minutes north of town. It was a small private airfield used mostly by recreational fliers on weekends and holidays. This being the Fourth of July weekend, it was as busy as a toy store on Christmas Eve.

hangared: stored in a large, barnlike building for aircraft

The weather was perfect for gliding. The sky was clear and the air temperature was in the mid-eighties. There was a steady ten-mile-per-hour wind blowing in from the west, and the humidity was right around sixty percent. I couldn't have asked for better conditions.

Mom and Dad had already arranged for the plane to be ready for us when we arrived. Climbing out of our car, I saw our glider, the *Sky Dancer*, sitting on the grass <u>tethered</u> to the single-engined tow plane that would lift it into the sky.

For those of you who've never seen a sailplane, they're incredibly beautiful, graceful creations. The *Sky Dancer*, for instance, had a narrow, bullet-shaped cockpit, much like a teardrop. Behind that, her <u>fuselage</u> extended back thirty-five feet, tapering into a thin, almost fragile-looking tail. Her wings spanned nearly forty feet, giving her the lift and stability she needed to stay aloft even without the benefit of a motor. Not designed for combat, transportation, carrying cargo, or any other practical concern, the *Sky Dancer* had one purpose and one purpose only: fun.

"Ready to go, Birthday Girl?" my father asked, giving me a warm pat on the shoulder.

"Let's do it," I said, fitting my helmet, which was painted metallic blue and covered with orange and red stars, over my head.

Five minutes later, I was belted into our sailplane's pilot seat. I gave my father a firm "thumbs-up," and he lowered the bubble-shaped cockpit hatch into place. My heart beating wildly, I watched my parents enter the tow plane parked about thirty feet in front of me. Then my helmet radio crackled into life.

tethered: tied to the end of a rope

fuselage: the body of a plane

"You reading me, Keisha?" my father asked.

"Loud and clear, Dad," I replied into my helmet's tiny microphone. "Let's get this baby in the air!"

Launching a sailplane is a relatively easy task. The tow plane does ninety percent of the work. As the glider pilot, all I had to do was release my brakes and let Dad and Mom use their rented plane to tow me onto the runway and up into the wild blue yonder. My only challenge was keeping my <u>rudder</u> straight.

A few minutes later, we were at almost 5,000 feet and traveling at about 100 miles per hour—slow for an airplane, but fast for a glider.

"Ready to solo, Birthday Girl?" Mom asked over the radio. "I'll bet you're excited!"

My hands were shaking and my throat suddenly felt dry. I took a deep breath, then answered back. "That's a big <u>ten-four</u>. Ready to release."

Releasing the towline was my job. Taking a deep breath, I reached forward and pulled the lever that disconnected my aircraft from the nylon <u>umbilical cord</u> connecting me to my parents' plane. I heard a clunk as the hook let go, then was thrown forward in my chair as the sailplane instantly <u>decelerated</u> by about twenty miles per hour. Looking straight ahead, I saw Mom and Dad's plane quickly pull away as it suddenly found itself free of its five-hundred-pound load.

Now I have to tell you there are many differences between riding in a sailplane as opposed to a regular, engine-powered aircraft. The first thing you notice right away is the sound. There isn't any. In a commercial jet—

**rudder:** a hinged piece of metal used to steer a plane

**ten-four:** OK

**umbilical cord:** a cord that connects an unborn baby to its mother

**decelerated:** slowed down

the kind most people fly in—there's always the dull roar of the engines in the background and a constant vibration you can feel in every bone in your body. In small, private planes, like the tow plane my mom and dad were in, the engines are so loud they're almost deafening, and the vibrations can be so bad they make your teeth chatter.

But sailplanes aren't like that. When you're in a glider, the silence is unreal. There's no roar of jets. No buzz of internal combustion engines. No vibrations to remind you that the only thing keeping you from tumbling to earth is this big, complicated machine with hundreds of parts, any one of which could fail.

## It's as if you, the sky, and the entire universe are one and the same.

This incredible silence was exactly what I was hearing as the tow plane circled back toward the airport and I was left to fly all on my own. For several moments, I just sat back and enjoyed the absolute nothingness of it all. This, I imagined, is what hawks must feel as they circle the skies in search of prey. It's as if you, the sky, and the entire universe are one and the same.

Sitting up, I turned my control wheel to the right, causing my sailplane to <u>bank</u> slightly in that direction. As it turned and I tilted sideways, I scanned the ground for

**bank:** to make a plane tilt to one side

Solo Flight    7

likely thermals, columns of warm air rising off the earth. It's these natural updrafts that allow glider pilots to keep themselves aloft for long periods of time even in gentle winds. Because darker areas—like parking lots—absorb sunlight and therefore heat the air around them, you always want to look for dark or paved patches of earth when flying a sailplane. Fly over one of these, and you can gain a few hundred feet without even trying.

As I mentioned earlier, this was a very bright, sunny day, so I had no problem finding all the thermals I needed. In fact, even after a full hour of circling the Sky Harbor area, I was still managing to keep the *Sky Dancer* at between 4,000 and 4,500 feet above sea level. Heck, the way things were going, I could probably stay aloft all the way till sundown if I wanted to. After that, the air would cool and I'd naturally find myself drifting back to earth.

However, my parents had no intention of letting me stay in the air that long. In fact, exactly one hour after the towline was released, my helmet radio came to life with the familiar sound of my father's voice.

"All right, Birthday Girl, it's time to bring *Sky Dancer* home," he said.

"Aw, Dad, do I have to?" I protested. I was having so much fun, I really didn't want to quit.

"We're going over to the Jacksons for a Fourth of July barbecue. Don't you remember?" he countered. "We're supposed to be there in an hour."

"Ten-four," I groaned in disappointment.

I adjusted my wing flaps to direct the sailplane earthward and at the same time began looking for bright patches of earth around which I'd find downdrafts to help bring me down.

Keeping a close eye on my <u>altimeter</u>, I suddenly noticed the oddest thing. No matter what I did to lower my <u>altitude</u>, the sailplane refused to descend below 4,000 feet!

"Come on, Keisha," my father said with some irritation. "I know you like it up there, but you can't stay there forever."

"I'm trying!" I radioed back. "But I seem to be caught in some kind of big thermal. I can't seem to lose altitude."

"Try to turn yourself out of it," my mother advised. "Look for bright patches of earth."

"That's what I'm doing!" I insisted.

Indeed, for the next fifteen minutes, I used every trick I knew to bring myself down, but nothing worked. In fact, I actually ended up gaining more than 200 feet!

---

**Hungry, thirsty, and desperately needing to go to the bathroom, I watched from my aerial perch as the sun sank with painful slowness below the western horizon, then finally vanished from sight.**

---

Now I was getting scared. All around me I could see other sailplanes rising and falling with no problem at all. At one point, Dad had a friend of his, who was also flying a glider, get in front of me and try to lead me home. Although *his* plane dropped without a problem, the *Sky*

**altimeter:** an instrument that measures altitude

**altitude:** height above the earth's surface

*Dancer* stayed exactly where she was.

"Dad, I don't know what to do," I radioed, my voice choked with panic. "What if I can't come down ever? What if I'm stuck up here for the rest of my life?"

"That's not going to happen," my father assured me. "There must be something wrong with your controls. If nothing else, we can wait till sunset."

And that's exactly what we had to do. For five full hours I circled around and around the Sky Harbor airport, becoming increasingly panicky with each passing minute. Hungry, thirsty, and desperately needing to go to the bathroom, I watched from my aerial perch as the sun sank with painful slowness below the western horizon, then finally vanished from sight. All the other gliders had long ago returned to the ground. I was now completely and utterly alone.

"The temperature's dropping really fast," my mother radioed. "It's already fallen ten degrees in the last hour. You should be down in no time."

Hearing this, I banked the *Sky Dancer* as tightly as I could and tried my hardest to put the sailplane into a spiraling dive. But, just as before, the craft absolutely refused to drop below 4,000 feet.

*I'm going to be up here forever!* I thought, terrified out of my mind. *A hundred years from now, I'll finally come down, and all they'll find in the cockpit is an old rotting skeleton!*

An hour later, the sky around me was a sea of stars set against a backdrop of inky blackness. I'd never been in a sailplane at night before—this kind of flying usually wasn't done—and the sense of complete isolation could easily

**PREDICT**

*What will happen to Keisha? Will she land her plane? Or will she become a flying corpse?*

drive a person insane. At least in an airplane you always had the noise of the engines to keep your senses stimulated. But up here in a sailplane, with no noise, no light, and virtually no sense of movement, you could quickly begin to feel totally disconnected from any sense of reality.

In fact, I was certain I was going stark raving mad when, gazing out through the bubble cockpit, I saw two eyes staring back at me. Chilled to the bone, I first told myself that I was either looking at my own reflection in the Plexiglas, or that I was seeing some distorted reflection of the full moon. The problem was, there *was* no moon shining this night, and the eyes were part of a face that was definitely not my own.

As I continued to examine the face gazing back at me, I saw that it belonged to a man in his mid-thirties. His hair was cut in the style of a military crewcut, and his uniform collar bore the bronze oak leaves of an Air Force major.

It took me a moment or two to realize that I'd seen this face before. In fact, it looked out from several framed photographs back home. It was the face of my very own grandfather.

"What are you doing here?" I asked the ghostly image floating before me. "What do you want from me?"

But rather than respond, the transparent face just continued to hang in the air outside my cockpit. It seemed to be looking through me, just as I was looking through it, and for a brief moment, I wondered which of us was truly the ghost.

Unable to stare at this frightening visage any longer, I glanced down at my controls and saw that I was still

**Plexiglas:** hard, transparent plastic

holding level at 4,000 feet. And then, as if waking up from a dream, I realized what was happening. My grandfather's spirit was holding me aloft. Maybe it thought it was helping me, or maybe it wanted me to join it in the vast beyond, there was no way to tell. I only knew that I had to get it to release me or I could indeed be stuck up here for the rest of my life.

"Grandfather, it's your granddaughter, Keisha," I said, struggling to remain calm. "You have to let me go. I want to go home. I want to see my mom and dad. They're worried sick about me. I don't want to die up here. Please, Grandfather, release me."

But the image just continued staring at me, and my altimeter refused to budge. What more could I do?

And then I noticed something about the spirit's uniform. There was something odd about it. Something was missing. The pilot's wings!

I immediately looked down at the wings pinned to my shirt. Could these be what my grandfather wanted? Could these be why he was keeping me aloft?

Hands shaking, I carefully removed the wings from my shirt. There was no response from the plane. I set the wings down on the floor. Still no change. Finally, I checked my seat belt to make sure the buckle was secure, then unlatched the cockpit <u>canopy</u> and opened it just a crack.

Instantly, a burst of freezing-cold wind hit me in the face, and the shock almost caused me to lose my grip. But I held fast and, with my free hand, scooped the pin off the floor and—sad as I was to lose this one solid reminder of my grandfather's greatness—I tossed the wings out into the

**canopy:** a covering

night. I saw them glisten in the starlight for a few brief seconds. Then they vanished from sight.

I released the cockpit canopy and let it fall back into place. Then I locked it securely and made sure it wasn't about to come loose. Finally, I glanced back at the front of the cockpit bubble . . . and saw that my grandfather's face had vanished!

Excited, I glanced at my altimeter and saw that the needle was starting to drop—4,000 feet . . . 3,950 feet . . . 3,900 feet . . .

"Sky Harbor control, this is *Sky Dancer*!" I said into my radio. "I'm coming home."

Just then the sky around me lit up with a blinding flash. A ball of fire seemed to be heading right for me . . . then seconds later, it disappeared. Stunned, I wondered if I'd just seen my grandfather's angry ghost.

And then it hit me.

"Fireworks," I said to myself with relief. "It's the Fourth of July fireworks!"

The sky around me continued to explode with joyous celebration as I continued my rapid descent. And then, as I turned on my final approach to the Sky Harbor runway, I saw, for the briefest instant, my grandfather's image within the glow of the display's grand <u>finale</u>. His pilot's wings were now pinned proudly to his chest. For the first time, he seemed to be smiling. As I smiled back, the glow from the fireworks faded out, and my grandfather's ghost disappeared forever.

**finale:** the last part of a public performance

# Solo Flight

### ▼ Learning from the Story

Have you ever had a trip turn out as bad as Keisha's? Compare awful trips and vacations with several other students by playing "How Bad Was It?" Go around the group and take turns completing the following sentences.

*You:   My trip to _____ was so bad!*

*Others:   How bad was it?*

*You:   It was so bad that . . . .*

One of these awful trips might just become the inspiration for your own disastrous travel story!

### ▼ Putting It into Practice

Create a travel brochure describing one of your own disastrous vacations or trips. Be sure to identify all the great things you could have done as well as everything that went wrong on the trip. Don't be afraid to exaggerate a little—or a lot!

# A "TRUE" Story

**Sometimes real life is even more terrifying than a good spooky story!**

ark tossed the branch he had been playing with onto the fire. "All right," he said to the other students, "I've got one."

Mark and his classmates were on the Keystone Middle School's annual spring trip. This year the class had elected to go camping in the forested mountains of the Colorado Rockies. They had piled into a school bus early one Saturday morning and had driven most of the day to reach the campground, now dotted with several multicolored tent domes.

Although there were two teachers along for supervision, the boys who had been lucky enough to come were mostly left on their own. The teachers' tents were a good fifty feet away—far enough from the students to give them the feeling of independence.

Now Mark and his buddies were taking advantage of their freedom. They were staying up long after the teachers had hit their sleeping bags and were sitting around the campfire, trying to terrify each other with the scariest stories they could think of.

Kurt and Felix had already told some pretty <u>petrifying</u> ones, but Mark felt sure his would really rattle their wits. "I won't tell you how I heard about this," he began, his face <u>eerily</u> lit by the dancing flames of the fire, "but I will promise that what I'm about to tell you is a true story."

Kurt snorted, but was promptly hushed by the others. They had a "golden rule," which stated that each storyteller had to be given a fair chance, so Mark just ignored Kurt and began.

"There was this kid," he said in a hushed tone. "We'll call him Mike. He lived alone with his dad at the edge of town, real close to the forest where his dad was working as a lumberjack.

"Sometimes Mike's dad would be gone for a few days when he was working deep in the forest, so Mike learned how to take care of himself. He wasn't afraid of the woods like a lot of the other kids. In fact, he was always goofing around among the huge trees, setting traps and fishing and stuff. Pretty soon, he knew his way around the woods better than most anyone else."

For a moment, Mark looked over his shoulder at the woods behind him for dramatic effect. Then he continued in an eerie tone.

"Anyway, one night when his dad was gone, Mike was sitting out on his front porch. He was staring up at the sky through his telescope when all of a sudden he saw a falling star. He watched it shoot across the sky, and then he realized he could track it with his telescope. He was following the fiery blaze, watching it fall closer and closer to earth, when it actually got close enough that he didn't

**petrifying:** paralyzing with fear

**eerily:** strangely, weirdly

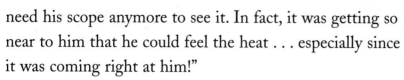

need his scope anymore to see it. In fact, it was getting so near to him that he could feel the heat . . . especially since it was coming right at him!"

"Bam!" yelled Kurt, clapping his hands together sharply.

The boy sitting next to him jumped, and everyone else laughed and poked the poor guy in the ribs. Then Felix, the class science genius, had to step in and ruin the mood by opening his big mouth.

"You know that's not really possible," Felix said. "Actually, I happen to know a lot about shooting stars. Did you know that according to—"

"Fee-lix!" the other boys shouted him down. "Nobody wants a science lecture now."

"Are you guys through?" Mark said, pretending to be the adult in the group. He rolled his eyes and tapped his foot impatiently. Then, only after everybody had settled down, he finally resumed his story.

"When Mike saw this thing flaming down out of the sky, he jumped for cover—and just in time. The <u>meteor</u> slammed into the ground about a hundred yards away. There was a huge flash of light and the sound of hundreds of trees snapping like pencils. Then everything got real quiet.

"Well, Mike didn't wait a single second. He took off running toward where he had seen the thing come down. But it was weird—there were no flames in sight. Still, it wasn't hard for Mike to locate. All he had to do was follow the disgusting smell—not of fire, but of something kind of like burning rubber.

**meteor:** a mass of stone or metal from outer space that speeds toward Earth

"Within minutes, he reached the crash site. It was awesome. The trees were all smashed up like twigs, and in the middle of the clearing was this huge pile of dirt that had been pushed up like a wave. Smoke was coming from the dirt, and Mike decided to get closer for a better look at what he was sure was a meteor.

"Except it wasn't a meteor. It was something silvery that kind of glowed in the dark." Mark paused for a moment, then said practically in a whisper, "It was a spaceship."

Felix <u>guffawed</u>. "Yeah, right. And you said this was a true story."

Once again everyone chorused "Fee-lix!" until the <u>bespectacled</u> future scientist gave up and let Mark go on.

## Mark paused for a moment, then said practically in a whisper, "It was a spaceship."

"Well, needless to say, Mike couldn't believe what he saw," Mark began again. "So he slid down the pile of dirt until he was actually standing on the ship itself. The surface was shiny, smooth, and warm to the touch. Mike figured a lot of it was buried underground since it didn't look very big.

"Anyway, he was standing there, wondering what to do, when suddenly he heard a faint knocking sound. At first he thought it was the sound of the surface of the ship

**PREDICT**

*What do you think will happen next?*

**guffawed:** laughed loudly

**bespectacled:** wearing glasses

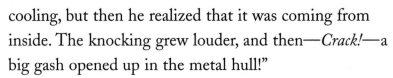

cooling, but then he realized that it was coming from inside. The knocking grew louder, and then—*Crack!*—a big gash opened up in the metal hull!"

Everybody flinched and the guy that Kurt had scared earlier gave a tiny yelp. The others teased him unmercifully, but Mark knew they were just trying to laugh off their own fright. He jumped up and started to walk around as he continued telling his story.

"The crack grew wider and wider until it made a circular hole. Then a horrible smell rolled out of the opening—it reminded Mike of the time he had found a rotting rabbit in a forgotten trap. It stunk so bad, Mike's legs went all rubbery, and he was shaking so much he could barely stand.

"Finally the crack stopped getting wider, so Mike inched his way closer to what was obviously some kind of doorway. His heart pounded so hard it practically made his shirt jump up and down, and the night seemed very quiet all of a sudden. He reached the edge of the opening and slowly leaned forward. Inch by inch, his head poked over the edge. He licked his lips, now dry with fear and excitement. He was going to be famous. He was going to be the first human ever to meet an <u>alien</u>!"

Mark looked around at his audience. He really had them, but knew he'd better get to the scary part pretty soon. He went on, trying to make his voice sound <u>ominous</u> and spooky.

"First Mike saw some blinking lights on the inside wall. Next, he saw something that looked like a tunnel into the center of the ship. He leaned a little farther . . . and there it was—a dark shape lying in the middle of the tunnel.

**PREDICT**

*Was your first prediction correct? Now what do you think will happen?*

**alien:** a strange being from another planet

**ominous:** threatening

"Suddenly a tentacle shot out! Before Mike could scream, it wrapped around his throat. He tried to get away, but the slimy thing was too strong for him. Gasping for breath, he felt himself being pulled over the edge of the hole and into the ship. The thing—a hideous cross between a spider and an octopus—had him . . . and it was pulling him closer to its mouth!"

Mark held his hands about a foot apart. "Mike was this close to going down the gross thing's ugly, slimy throat. In fact, he was so close he almost passed out from the <u>stench</u> of the thing's breath. Then its tongue—with millions of tiny teeth right on it—snaked out. It swirled across Mike's face like sandpaper, tearing into his cheeks and practically ripping off his nose. Then, just before he blacked out, Mike saw small tentacles ooze out of the alien's head. Although he tried, he couldn't fight off the alien as it sank one of its tentacles right into his skull and bored through it like it was a coconut, heading straight for his brain."

Mark paused while his audience made appropriate sounds of disgust. Then, before they had time to speak, he held up his hand.

"Wait a minute. There's more. You see, some time later Mike woke up. But he wasn't exactly *Mike* anymore. The alien had taken over, or assimilated, his body . . . *and* his life."

"What?" one of the boys gasped.

"That's right. Once it was comfortable in its new body, the alien set the ship to self-destruct. Then it followed Mike's memories back to the house where he had grown up. There it waited for its new human parent—Mike's dad—to return.

**stench:** terrible smell

"And the worst part of the whole story is that poor Mike, even though he didn't have a body anymore, still had enough consciousness to know what was happening. He figured out that the alien would take over his dad, too, and that the more humans it assimilated, the more capable it was of reproducing itself over and over again. In time it would control the planet. And all Mike could do was watch in silent horror, knowing that he had brought about the doom of the human race."

Mark's voice dropped to a whisper as he finished, and he stood still in the flickering shadows cast by the <u>waning</u> campfire. The stunned silence was everything he could have hoped for. He waited as his classmates slowly began breathing again.

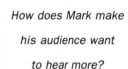

How does Mark make his audience want to hear more?

A boy named Malcolm sighed heavily. "It's like that movie where the scientists are at the South Pole and they find an alien that takes people over and makes copies of them." The boy shivered. "Afterward, the scientists couldn't tell who was real and who was a copy."

Kurt rolled his eyes. Of course *he* had to be the one to try to knock Mark's story down. Kurt was always the first to have something negative to say.

"I thought you said it was a true story," he accused. "That story was no more true than a fairy tale."

Mark looked at him innocently. "It *is* true."

Kurt shook his head. "Uh, uh. No way."

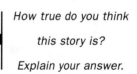

How true do you think this story is? Explain your answer.

Mark tried not to smile. Someone just had to figure it out. In fact, he had been betting on it. "Okay, smart guy," he challenged Kurt, "why is there no way it can be true?"

"There's no way because there was nobody around when the kid went into the spaceship," Kurt said,

waning: dying out

pouncing on what he was sure was the flaw in Mark's logic. "And if the kid never came out, and the alien blew up the ship, then there's nobody to tell the story and no evidence that the ship or the alien ever existed."

"That's true," Mark admitted. "But you missed one important point."

Everyone listened closely to see how he would defend himself.

"There *is* one person who knows the whole story," Mark said, nearly whispering, "but his name isn't Mike."

Suddenly Mark pulled open his shirt. "It's me!" he yelled as thick, black tentacles shot out from his chest.

Everyone screamed. It looked like a grenade had exploded in the middle of the circle as the boys jumped, crawled, or rolled backward away from the monster who had once been Mark.

"What is it?" yelled the teachers as they came racing over from their tents.

Mark knelt in front of the fire, nearly breathless with laughter. Tears streamed down his face as he propped himself with his hands to keep from falling over. The tentacles now bounced and swayed gently at his side, looking suspiciously like black nylons stuffed with something springy.

"What's going on?" demanded Mr. Owens, the English teacher.

Mark managed to catch his breath and tried to answer, but the sight of his classmates slowly picking themselves up made him break out laughing once again.

"Ah, nothing, Mr. Owens," said Mark's best friend, Zack, who had kept quiet throughout Mark's story.

"Nothing?" repeated Mr. DeRocha, the science teacher. "You were all screaming like it was the end of the world!"

Mark finally recovered enough to explain. "You see, we were telling scary stories, and I guess mine was a little too scary."

The teachers—hands on hips—studied the group of kids. Everyone was trying to look as if it had been somebody else screaming and not them.

"Nothing?" repeated Mr. DeRocha, the science teacher. "You were all screaming like it was the end of the world!"

Finally Mr. Owens pronounced that it was late and that everyone had to be in their tents—*asleep*—within the next fifteen minutes.

Most of the kids were still too embarrassed to do anything but agree. Some of them shot Mark dirty looks, but others grinned or gave him the thumbs-up sign, wishing they had been as clever as he was.

True to Mr. Owens's wishes, fifteen minutes later they were all in their tents, although not exactly asleep. The sound of whispered conversations and muffled laughter could be heard from every tent.

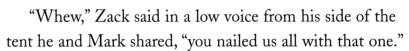

"Whew," Zack said in a low voice from his side of the tent he and Mark shared, "you nailed us all with that one."

Mark smiled. "You know, I think Nigel almost had a heart attack."

Zack clutched his chest and fell backward. The two boys burst into giggles and spent the next few minutes making jokes about who had been the most scared of the group.

After their laughing fit had passed, Zack leaned over close to Mark. "Where did you get that story from, anyway?" he asked in a whisper.

"Why?" Mark whispered back.

"I mean, did you get it from that movie Malcolm was talking about?"

"What makes you think I made it up?" Mark asked, suddenly serious.

Zack was silent a moment. Then he said in an angry tone, "Come on, Mark. I really want to know where you got the story. Stop goofing around."

Mark didn't answer right away. The silence in the tent seemed to take on a life of its own. Finally the breath Mark had been holding in exploded out of his mouth in a bark of laughter. "Of course I made it up! What do you think—it really happened?"

There was a strange sound from Zack, as if his sleeping bag was being torn open. "Good," he sneered as he clamped a hand tightly over Mark's mouth. "I was worried for a moment that I'd been discovered."

# A "TRUE" Story

### ▼ Learning from the Story

The plot of a story includes the events, or "steps" a story takes to get from beginning to end. Work with three or four of your classmates to map out the events in this story. Go around the group. Have the first person identify the first event in the story and write it on a notecard. The next person identifies the next event and writes it on his or her card. Continue until you have cards for all the events in the story. Then lay the cards out in order.

Look over the cards. Pull out any cards that describe the events in Mark's story about the aliens. This is a story within a story, a plot within the plot. Notice how both plots begin by introducing characters and setting. How does each plot end?

### ▼ Putting It into Practice

Look back over your own story ideas. Which has the makings of a great disastrous travel story? Try to plot out that story.

- Fold a sheet of paper three times. Label one end The Beginning, the other The End.
- Use these sections of the paper to start plotting out how your story might start and end.
- In the folds in between, start identifying the steps you'll take to get from the beginning to the end.

# GHOST BRIDGE

Seeing is believing. But what happens when you stop believing?

"I'm just telling you what it says," said Jake's mom, not looking up from the travel book. "A tornado destroyed the bridge in 1979, and it hasn't been rebuilt yet."

"Well, that's awfully funny," said his father in that patient voice he used just before he was about to lose his temper, "because we're halfway across the bridge now."

They were on a trip to visit Jake's grandparents, who lived over three states away. It was the longest car trip they had ever taken together.

Jake glanced out the back window of the moving car, and his eyes widened. He wasn't sure if he believed his own eyes, so he whispered to his little sister, Drew, "Look out the back window and let me know if you see anything weird."

Drew obediently looked out and gasped. The bridge was disappearing right behind them, as if it were dissolving seconds after they drove over it!

Jake's mother continued to read from the travel book. "Apparently there's a local legend about the bridge," she said. "It says here that once in a while, people do see the bridge. It appears just as it did before it was destroyed, and it <u>lures</u> unwary travelers . . ." Her voice trailed off.

"Where?" asked Jake's dad. "Where does it lure unwary travelers? Where?"

"Just hurry, Dad," Jake said quickly. "Get us over it."

"Come *on*, Dad," Drew begged. "Step on it!"

"Just drive," said their mother tightly, closing the book and shutting her eyes. "Just drive."

# "No!
# Keep driving!
## *Don't slow down!*"

Jake's dad looked across the front seat at her, then he glanced back at Jake's and Drew's anxious faces. "Well, if this family isn't acting ridiculous," he said. "I have half a mind to pull over right now to talk this out."

The three of them all spoke at once. "No! Keep driving! *Don't slow down!*"

"What does the book say, exactly?" Jake's dad was getting annoyed. "Now that you started it, I want to know."

His mom opened the book and read the rest of the legend. "It lures unwary travelers to their deaths. But when someone believes in the ghost bridge—really *believes* that it exists—he or she will make it to the other side."

**lures:** attracts; tempts

"That's it?" asked Jake's dad, grinning.

"That's it," said his mom, closing the book once more.

"Well, as I figure it," his dad said smugly, "since there are three people in this car who *don't* believe in the bridge, it's all up to me to get us to the other side."

They drove on in tense silence.

"Hmmm . . . that's funny," he said after a few moments. "There *is* something strange about this bridge. It's almost as if I can see the bottom of the canyon through it." He paused and glanced at the family. "You don't think that maybe . . ."

*Don't think that!* Drew wanted to cry out.

*Just keep going!* Jake wanted to shout.

*Don't start listening to us now!* their mom wanted to yell.

But it was too late. All that came out were their screams as the car <u>plummeted</u> to the canyon floor far below.

**plummeted:** plunged; dropped

# GHOST BRIDGE

## ▼ Learning from the Story

How much of this story do you learn through the dialogue? To find out, work with three other students. Assign each student a part in the story: Mom, Dad, Jake, or Drew. Go through the story. Have each student read only his or her character's words. Skip over anything described by the narrator. Is any of the story left out? How much did you learn from the dialogue alone?

## ▼ Putting It into Practice

Think about the characters in your own disastrous travel story and the events you plotted out. How can you use dialogue to move the plot along?

Describe the main characters in your story to your group. Choose an event from your plot and explain what is happening at this point in the story. Assign each person the role of a character. Have the characters act out the scene. Take notes on any dialogue that seems to work especially well. You may be able to use it in your story.

# Heart of
# STONE

**There are two kinds of people in this world:
those who aren't afraid of anything and those who
have the good sense to be afraid of everything!**

aster Sergeant Harold Stone, U.S. Marine
Corps, pulled the jeep to a stop and shut off
the motor. "Wake up, Joel," he said, shaking his
stepson awake.

Joel opened one eye. The sky was overcast, and pools of
mist clung to the ground. All he did was groan.

Harry opened his door and got out. Walking around to
the back of the jeep, he lifted the rear hatch, letting in a
blast of cold, damp air. "Out!" he ordered.

"What time is it?" Joel asked, rubbing his eyes.

"Five-thirty. Hit the deck, mister." Harry strapped a
backpack on over his <u>fatigues</u> and held one out to Joel.

Joel took the backpack reluctantly, climbed out of the
jeep, and stood beside it, looking around in the early
morning light. Harry had parked by the edge of a forest,
but in the distance Joel could see the deserted slopes of the
Mammoth ski area in northern California.

It was late May—too late for skiers and too early for
summer vacationers. The jeep was the only vehicle in
sight. A nearby sign read "Inyo National Forest," and an

**fatigues:** work clothes
worn by soldiers

arrow below pointed the way through the woods to the Devil's Postpile Ranger Station.

It had begun to drizzle, and Joel shivered, pulling his jacket hood over his head and groaning again. He knew it promised to be a dismal day in more ways than one.

Bareheaded, Harry looked skyward. "A little water never hurt anybody," he said. "Like I've been telling your mother, you need to toughen up." Slinging a thirty-foot safety rope over his shoulder, he turned to his stepson impatiently. "Move it, Joel. We've got a long walk ahead of us."

Joel sighed. "Where'd you say we're going?" he asked.

"The Devil's Postpile," Harry answered. "It's volcanic rock that formed thousands of years ago into columns that look like gigantic posts." He strode briskly into the forest, following the trail toward the ranger station. "Now, save your breath. You'll need it at this altitude."

*I should have never let Mom talk me into this*, Joel thought, trotting after him.

The two traveled in silence until the path ended and they emerged into a clearing where they found the ranger's shack. "You just caught me," she said, coming out the door, looking surprised. "We don't get many people here this time of year. You're not thinking about heading into the Devil's Postpile, are you?"

"Yeah, we are," Harry said. "Is there a problem?"

"I need to warn you that the trail may have been made unsafe by all the recent earthquake activity in the area," the ranger said. She pointed toward a stand of pine trees. "You really don't have to go up there. You can see the Postpile from here."

Joel looked to where the ranger pointed and saw a wall of rock columns about a half mile away, its ridge covered by low-lying clouds.

"The wall of the Devil's Postpile rises sixty feet, and some of the rock is crumbling from natural erosion," the ranger went on. "But with all the <u>seismic</u> activity we had during the winter, I wouldn't recommend hiking up there."

"You have earthquakes here, too?" Joel asked, looking around anxiously. "I—I've had just about enough of them."

Joel and his mom used to live in southern California, near the <u>epicenter</u> of the big quake that struck the San Fernando Valley in 1994. It was not an experience Joel wanted to repeat. Luckily, after his mom married Harry, they moved to Oregon. Moving away from what Joel called "Earthquake Valley" was the only thing he'd found positive about his mother's marriage to Harry Stone—a man who treated him more like a recruit than a stepson.

The ranger smiled warmly at Joel. "I see you've got a healthy fear of shakers," she said. "Well, we've only had a couple of minor shocks around here. No more than 3.5 on the <u>Richter scale</u>." She paused for a moment, then looked at Harry. "Look, if you and your boy here are good hikers, I'd say you could make it. But I'd be careful." She got into her truck. "I've got rounds to make. Have fun."

"Thanks," Harry said. "I've been here before, but we'll be extra careful."

"Fine," the ranger said. Fishing around in her glove compartment, she came out with a receipt book. "In that case, I need to collect a seven-dollar park fee from you."

**seismic:** having to do with earthquakes

**epicenter:** the point directly above the center of an earthquake

**Richter scale:** a system for measuring the strength of an earthquake

"Seven bucks," Harry grumbled, reaching for his wallet. "What if we'd missed you?"

The ranger smiled and took the money. "Well, I guess you wouldn't have paid," she said, handing Harry a receipt. "This must be your lucky day!"

The ranger started her truck, then leaned out the window. "Just one more thing," she said as she started to drive off. "The wildlife up around the Postpile has all but disappeared lately. Probably doesn't mean a thing, but animals do have a sense about things, you know. Anyway, if you see anything unusual, I'd leave if I were you."

Joel looked after the departing truck nervously. "Maybe we should hike someplace else. What if the animals are sensing an earthquake?"

"Listen, mister, you've got to stop using earthquakes as an excuse," Harry said. "Your mom and I talked about it, and we think you need to overcome your fears."

"That's easy for you to say," Joel grumbled. "You weren't there."

"Maybe not, but I know it'd take more than an earthquake to scare me," his stepdad said. "Harry Stone didn't get the nickname 'Heart of Stone' in the Marine Corps for nothing." And with that he turned on his heels and marched rapidly into the woods.

What kind of person is Harry Stone?

It had quit raining by the time the two reached the base of the rock formation known as the Devil's Postpile. Joel had to admit it was pretty cool as he stared at the postlike trunks of stone. Some stood upright or leaned at odd angles, while others appeared to have been gathered by a giant hand and thrown around like pickup sticks. The sheer rock wall of stone posts towered over the area like a dark sentinel. <u>Mesmerized</u> by the ominous towers of volcanic rock, Joel shuddered. With its head hidden in the clouds and a white vapor rising from around its base, the Devil's Postpile definitely gave off an eerie feeling.

"That's weird," Joel said, looking at the ground. A steamlike mist was rising from the rocks beneath his feet as well. Kneeling, he touched one of the rocks. "Hey, Harry. This rock feels awfully warm. How can that be? The sun has been hidden behind clouds all day."

Harry shrugged, then grinned. "Well, they say the Devil's Postpile is a tourist hot spot!" he said with a laugh.

Joel rolled his eyes. "I'm serious, Harry."

"I'm serious, too," Harry said. "I'm serious about not letting you let your fears consume you. Now, let's keep hiking, shall we?" Turning, he started off at an even quicker pace than before, picking his way over and around the log-shaped rocks with ease.

His curiosity aroused, Joel followed at a much slower pace. Clearly the evaporation of rainwater on the heated surface of the rocks was what caused the steamy effect. But what made the rocks hot? Closely studying the ground beneath his feet, he stopped at intervals to feel the surface of the rock. It was warm all over, but some places seemed hotter than others. In fact, at one point when Joel tripped and put his hand onto a large boulder to steady himself, he actually got scorched.

**mesmerized:** fascinated

"Ouch!" he yelped, shaking his hand to cool it off.

"What the heck's the matter now?" Harry snapped.

"I'm telling you, Harry," Joel said. "There *is* something weird about this place. Feel this rock."

"I'm not feeling any rocks," Harry said flatly. "And I don't want to hear any excuses from you. We're going up to the top, or my nickname isn't Heart of Stone!"

*Boy, does that name ever fit*, Joel thought. Then he yelled aloud to Harry, "I'm not making up an excuse! There's really something strange going on here, and I think we should leave. You heard what the ranger said about the animals. I think they left because they know something's going to happen."

"Listen," Harry replied sternly, "I told your mother I'd take you for a mountain hike, and that's exactly what I'm going to do." He took the rope from his shoulder and quickly tied one end around his waist. "Tie this around your waist. I'm going to make sure you keep up with me."

Joel sighed and did as he was told. There was no arguing with Heart of Stone Harry. "How long are we going to have to hike like this?" he asked.

"Until we get to the top," Harry replied. Then he turned, gave the rope a pull, and started up the trail, dragging Joel behind him like a cowboy with a roped steer.

"Wait!" Joel protested, stumbling along in the increasingly growing mist. "Can't we talk about this?"

But Harry didn't answer. In minutes he had already gone the distance of the rope, and Joel couldn't even see him in the mist. It was like walking inside a thick cloud.

"Hey, come on, Harry! Slow down!" Joel protested. "I can't walk or even see—"

*If you were Joel, what would you do?* ▶

But Joel's sentence was cut short when Harry let out a deafening scream. Then, in the same moment, the rope around Joel's waist jerked with such force that it brought him to his knees, gasping in pain.

"Harry!" Joel called. "Are you all right?"

There was no answer.

Frightened, Joel scrambled to his feet and began pulling on the rope that was now completely slack. When there was no more rope to pull on, Joel found himself holding nothing but a frayed end.

"Harry?" he called, his voice hollow as he staggered blindly ahead in a mist so thick he couldn't see two feet in front of him. "Where are you? Are you OK?"

Once again Harry didn't answer, and Joel started to fear the worst. Either Harry was injured or he was playing tricks on him, waiting to spring out of the mist and scare him half to death.

---

**"Harry?" he called, his voice hollow as he staggered blindly ahead in a mist so thick he couldn't see two feet in front of him. "Where are you? Are you OK?"**

---

His heart pounding, Joel froze and strained to hear Harry's footsteps, but the only sound he heard was the chatter of his own teeth. Then suddenly the trail ended, and squinting through the mist, Joel saw a huge gash in the earth . . . too late.

Stumbling into the opening and turning his ankle, Joel was unable to catch himself before he slid into the large <u>crevice</u>, banging his head hard against the rock. Instantly brilliant stars danced before his eyes . . . and then everything went black.

✳ ✳ ✳

When he came to, Joel was lying on the floor of an underground <u>cavern</u>. A misty vapor rose from holes in the rock floor, warming the air around him. Groaning, he sat up and sniffed the air. Something smelled like rotten eggs.

*Sulfur*, Joel thought. *I have to get out of here. But how?*

Looking up, he could see light shining down through the crevice where he had fallen. It was only a few yards above him, and the angle of the <u>incline</u> didn't seem too steep. Joel figured he could climb out. At least he knew he had to try.

Struggling to his feet, Joel grimaced from the pain in his ankle. Then, resolving to save himself, he started to climb, when he heard his name coming from deep within the dark cavern.

"Harry!" Joel cried in relief. "Where are you?"

"Over here!" Harry called. "Hurry!"

Limping in the direction of his stepdad's voice, Joel found him a few yards away, buried up to his neck in a pit of black goo. "What happened?" Joel gasped.

"Looks like we both fell into the same underground cavern," Harry said. "I wasn't hurt, so I decided to take a quick look around and stepped into this stuff. It looked solid

**crevice:** a narrow crack

**cavern:** a large cave

**incline:** a slanting surface

when I stepped into it, but it sure sucked me down like quicksand."

"I'll go for help," Joel said.

"No, I think you can pull me out," Harry insisted. "The rope is still tied to my waist. Grab hold of that frayed end and start tugging."

Joel found where the yellow nylon rope emerged from the black goo and pulled on it with all his might. But Harry didn't budge.

"Look, Harry, it's no use. I'm going for help," Joel said after a few more unsuccessful attempts.

"Okay, but hurry," Harry said, beginning to sweat. "Whatever this stuff is, it seems to be getting hotter."

For a moment Joel hesitated. "I don't know how long it'll take to find somebody," he said. "Will you—"

"Just go," Harry snapped. Then his face broke into a wide grin. "And you don't need to tell me to stay put."

Joel smiled at his stepdad. He could tell Harry was more frightened than he wanted to let on.

Ignoring the pain in his ankle, Joel rapidly scaled the incline to the path above. Emerging in the open, he took a deep breath of fresh air. A lot of the heavy mist had burned off and the sun was almost directly above him now. From his vantage point, he could see several miles in every direction. Shading his eyes, Joel looked for a sign of life but saw no one.

Then he heard the distant whine of a chain saw and turned to look in the direction of the sound. A few miles away he could see a group of forestry trucks gathered around a stand of pine trees.

*Has your opinion of Harry changed? What about your opinion of Joel?*

"Harry!" he called, leaning into the crevice. "I see someone. Hang in there. I'll have you outta there in no time."

The path beneath his feet was covered with loose rocks, and Joel had trouble keeping his balance as he slid downhill toward the trucks. With his ankle hurting terribly, he still kept going until finally he'd reached the bottom of the trail . . . and that's when he heard it.

Beginning with a low rumble, deep in the <u>bowels</u> of the earth, the ground beneath Joel's feet began to tremble, then abruptly stopped. *Earthquake!* his mind screamed.

Frozen with terror, he waited for the aftershock, afraid to step in any direction. But before he could even think about moving, Joel heard a loud explosion, and the flat surface of the rock around him <u>disintegrated</u> before his eyes. Then, to his horror and amazement, a fountain of volcanic lava erupted beneath his feet.

For a second he thought he heard Harry—old Heart of Stone—scream. But Joel didn't have time to worry about the man, or even to worry about himself. All he had time to do was let out an <u>ironic</u> laugh as he thought the last thing he would ever think: *Too bad Harry won't be able to report back to my mom that I'm not afraid of earthquakes anymore,* Joel's tortured mind mused. *Now I'm afraid of volcanoes!*

**bowels:** the inner part

**disintegrated:** crumbled; fell apart

**ironic:** strangely funny

# Heart of
# STONE

## ▼ Learning from the Story

Can you tell who said something just by the words they choose? Play "Who Said That?" with several other students. Have one student read a quotation from one of the characters in "Heart of Stone." The rest of the group should try to guess who said it. Think about why a word or phrase is uniquely Harry's or Joel's. What is the difference between the two of them?

## ▼ Putting It into Practice

Think about the main character in your own story. What words or phrases would be uniquely his or hers? Fold a sheet of paper in half. Label one half "She's (he's) always saying" and list two or three phrases that capture the unique personality of your character. Label the other half "She'd (he'd) never say" and list two or three phrases that would never come out of this character's mouth.

# The Good Deed

Cory wandered down to the edge of the lake to stare at the water. Behind him, he could hear his two sisters shouting as they chased each other around the campsite. Across the lake, he could see his dad wading thigh-deep in the cold lake water, casting his fishing line out onto the still surface. His mom was reading under the shade of a tree, not too far from where his father was catching dinner.

Cory sighed and flopped down on the coarse grass that fringed the shores of the lake. He had always enjoyed coming on these camping trips with his family. But this time something felt different. He felt, well, kind of bored. After all, why should he be hanging around with his family? He was going into junior high in September. None of the other guys would be caught dead taking a trip with their families anymore.

"Yep," Cory said out loud to no one, "I'm getting too old for this kind of thing."

Realizing that there was nothing he could do about it now, he got to his feet and set off on a tour of the lake. Maybe he'd find something interesting. He caught his dad's

Think about a time you did something good, really good—only to have that good deed turn into a huge, huge mistake. What happened?

attention and waved his arm in a circle, indicating the path around the lake. His dad nodded and waved back. *Good,* Cory thought. *At least he's not going to make me fish with him.*

This was the first time the family had been to this lake, so Cory took his time on the trail that wove along the shore. Fed by a number of small streams from the melting snow on the mountains that surrounded it, the lake lay in a bowl at the base of the towering peaks. At various points, clumps of pine trees grew right to the water's edge, and Cory had to kick his way through a thick carpet of pine needles. Sometimes the trail would disappear altogether, hidden by boulders that had tumbled down from the <u>eroded</u> peaks.

Cory tried hard to remain bored with everything, but he had to admit it was kind of fun, scrambling over the warm rocks, trying to sneak up on lizards basking in the sun.

At one point Cory climbed over a large pile of boulders and found himself on the arm of a small, sheltered bay. The water was as still as glass there, and he stared at the reflection of sky and mountains that came off of it. Then he picked up a rock and, with one swift throw, instantly shattered the image. *Maybe it'll scare the fish toward Dad,* he thought as he descended into the tiny cove and made his way around it.

On the opposite side of the lake, Cory found a faint trail leading away from the water. It appeared to follow a narrow brook. "Maybe it's some kind of <u>game</u> trail," he muttered to himself. Curious, he decided to follow it.

The trail ran deep into the woods, hugging the brook's edge, but after a while it veered away from the

**eroded:** worn down

**game:** wild animals

water and zigzagged toward a clearing. On one side of the clearing was a cabin built of dark brown wood that rested on a base of large, gray rocks. Cory didn't see anyone around and, glancing at his watch, decided there wasn't enough time to check it out. *Besides,* he reasoned, *it's probably private property, anyway.* Quietly ducking back into the trees, he returned to the lakeside to finish his tour and get back to camp in time for dinner. Maybe he'd come back to explore the cabin before the end of the trip.

❋ ❋ ❋

"Going to do some fishing today?" his dad asked him the next morning after breakfast.

Cory shrugged. He hadn't really thought about it, but it seemed like a better choice than doing nothing. "Yeah, sure," he answered.

Cory fetched his rod and tackle so his dad could get the line ready with its red-and-white bobber and tiny golden hook. Then the two of them wandered down to the lake.

Nearly three hours later, Cory figured the fish must be laughing their <u>gills</u> off. Cory's dad had caught only one fish and Cory hadn't caught any. Discouraged, they returned to camp for lunch.

"Good thing we're not living off what Cory catches," his sister Kirsti teased.

"Yeah," his other sister, Nicole, agreed. "We'd starve to death."

Cory made a face at them and took another bite of his sandwich. He thought about the private bay he had

What's the significance of the cabin? Why did the author mention it?

gills: the body part a fish uses to breathe in water

found yesterday. *There've got to be fish in there,* he thought. "Oh yeah?" he said to his sisters. "Well, I bet I catch some fish this afternoon."

"What kind—goldfish?" Kirsti asked sarcastically.

------------

**"OK, but don't wander off**

**too far and get lost," his dad warned.**

**"It can get tricky out here,**

**and you could easily lose your way."**

------------

Nicole thought this was the funniest thing she'd heard during the whole trip and howled with laughter. Cory ignored the brats. "There's a place I want to try on the other side of the lake," he said to his dad. "I'll catch up with you later, OK?"

"OK, but don't wander off too far and get lost," his dad warned. "It can get tricky out here, and you could easily lose your way."

Cory nodded in agreement, wolfed down the rest of his lunch, and grabbed his fishing rod. Soon he was back at what he was beginning to think of as "his" cove. He climbed down the rocks to the water's edge and found a comfortable shelf of rock to sit on. He baited his hook and cast his line far out into the middle of the water. Then, letting the line rest on his finger so he could feel the tug of a hungry fish, Cory closed his eyes and relaxed.

Suddenly he heard a huge splash, and his eyes flew open. *I must have fallen asleep,* he thought. Looking at the

<u>horizon</u> he was surprised to see that the sun had already sunk so low it was touching the tops of the peaks to the west. He sat up and looked toward the water to see what had awakened him, and saw a small, inflatable boat floating toward shore. It was being pushed along on the waves created by someone frantically thrashing in the center of the bay. Seeing that it was a girl, Cory first thought it was one of his sisters.

*But we don't have a boat like that,* he quickly told himself. *And Kirsti and Nicole know how to swim. That girl looks like she's drowning!* Without another thought, Cory kicked off his tennis shoes and dove off the rocks into the water.

The cold hit him like a blow to the chest, and he came up gasping. Then, with a burst of energy, he knifed through the water toward the yellow rubber boat. He grabbed it by a rope that hung from its side and pulled it toward the frantic girl.

"Hang on!" he yelled. "I'm coming!"

She didn't seem to hear him over the sound of her own choking breath and kept flailing her arms in the air. Finally Cory reached her and grabbed one of her arms. Feeling another person nearby, the girl clenched her arm around Cory's neck in a death hold.

His breath practically choked off, Cory began to panic as the girl refused to loosen her grip. With no other choice, he punched the girl hard on her shoulder until he managed to jog her loose.

"Are you trying to kill me, too?" Cory gasped, reaching for the boat and pulling it toward them. "Here's the boat. Grab it!"

**PREDICT**

*Will Cory save the girl?*

**horizon:** the line where the earth seems to meet the sky

Her eyes wide, the terrified girl swung her arm over the edge of the boat and held on with a white-knuckled grip.

"All right," Cory said, breathing heavily while he helped keep the girl's head above water. "Can you climb in?"

The girl nodded. Then, with Cory's help, she slid over the side and into the small boat, followed by her exhausted savior.

For what seemed like ages, the two lay in the bottom of the boat, silently gasping. Finally Cory sat up. "Can you help me paddle this thing to shore?" he asked.

The girl took a few more breaths, then nodded. "I think so," she said.

Cory glanced around. "Looks like the oars are gone." He shrugged. "Oh, well. Let's get going."

They each took one side of the boat and paddled with their hands until it slowly slid across the cove to the small trail Cory had seen yesterday. When the boat's tip finally bounced against the shore, Cory thought it was the finest sound he'd ever heard. He quickly <u>clambered</u> out of the boat, and the girl followed him.

"Thank you," she said shyly. "You saved my life." She held out her hand. "My name's Sadie."

Cory shook her hand and introduced himself. "Well, I'm just glad you're all right," he said, a little embarrassed. "But tell me—how did you fall in? It's not exactly wavy out there."

Sadie looked up the trail in the direction of the cabin. "I'm here staying with my grandfather. While he was gone today, I decided to take the boat out. I'm not supposed to," she added, biting her lip. "You see, I can't swim. For some reason, my grandfather won't teach me."

**clambered:** climbed using both hands and feet

Cory shivered in the cool air of the late afternoon. The sun had now fallen behind the mountains, and the bay was completely in shadow. Sadie still hadn't answered his question, so he asked again. "But I still don't understand why you fell in."

"I'm not sure, either," Sadie said, shrugging. "I was bending over to look at something on the bottom of the lake, and I guess I lost my balance." She stopped for a moment and noticed Cory shivering. "Do you want to come up to the cabin? My grandfather should be back by now, and you could get warm by the fire."

Cory thought about his family around their own fire and hesitated for a moment, knowing he should get back. Then he figured, *Why not? They'll understand. After all, I'm a hero now.* "OK," he told Sadie. "I am kind of cold."

When they got to the cabin, Sadie's grandfather was indeed home, and he jumped up from the table when the two soaking kids came through the door.

"Sadie!" he exclaimed. "What happened to you?" He looked at Cory suspiciously.

Sadie threw herself into her grandfather's arms. "Grandpa," she said, her face buried in his sweater, "I'm sorry!"

The old man held her closely while Cory squirmed uncomfortably under his sharp blue eyes.

"For what, honey?" the man asked, his eyes still fixed on Cory.

"I know I'm not supposed to, but I took the boat out and it tipped over." She looked at Cory and pointed. "He saved me, Grandpa."

**PREDICT**

*Was your first prediction right? Why do you think Sadie really fell into the water?*

"What?" the man demanded, holding Sadie at arm's length and looking sternly at her. "You took the boat out on the lake?"

Sadie nodded tearfully. "I'm sorry, Grandpa. I'll never do it again."

"And you fell in," he said in the same tone. "You see how dangerous it is?"

"Yes," Sadie sniffed. "I would have drowned if it hadn't been for Cory."

Cory had been watching the man's face as it showed first surprise, then relief. Now he saw something that looked like fear.

Turning abruptly away from Sadie, her grandfather strode over to the window and looked outside. Night had come quickly after the sun had disappeared behind the mountains, and the clearing around the cabin was now almost fully dark. Muttering under his breath, the man began pacing from window to window, yanking them open in order to pull the shutters closed.

"Bolt the door," he ordered Sadie.

Seemingly as mystified as Cory by all this sudden activity, Sadie automatically obeyed.

"Excuse me, sir," Cory began, "but what's going on?"

"You foolish boy!" the man said angrily. "That was a nixie you snatched her from." He finished closing the last shutter and turned to face Cory angrily.

"A what?" asked Cory, completely confused and a little frightened by the man's behavior.

"A *nixie*," Sadie's grandfather repeated, as if that said it all. He made a visible effort to control himself, then explained further.

---

**The man's voice dropped lower.**

**"Nobody knows what they look like,**

**because they can change into**

**anything they want. But no matter what**

**shape they choose, they hate humans—**

**and will often try to kill them."**

---

"Nixies are ancient beings—as old as the hills, as old as the trees. They live in lakes, ponds—in *all* bodies of water." The man's voice dropped lower. "Nobody knows what they look like, because they can change into anything they want. But no matter what shape they choose, they hate humans—and will often try to kill them."

Cory didn't know whether to laugh at this wild talk or run in fear of the crazy old man. He looked helplessly at Sadie, who was standing beside the door and watching the whole scene very quietly. Something about her lack of reaction made Cory more nervous than anything else.

"Where I come from," the man continued in a husky voice, "it is said to be bad luck to save a drowning person.

Fate has offered that person to the nixie, who must have at least one human <u>sacrifice</u> per year."

"But that's crazy!" cried Cory. "You can't just stand by and let someone drown. Besides, if it hadn't been for me, your granddaughter would be dead."

The man brought his hands up to his face. "I know," he said, his voice muffled and strained with emotion. "And for saving her, I'm grateful."

Cory was afraid the old guy was going to burst into tears. He turned toward Sadie. "Listen," he said, "it's really late, and my folks are probably getting worried. I think I'd better go."

"I don't think that's a good idea," she said quietly.

Halfway to the door, Cory stopped. A terrible thought rose up from the depths of his mind and seized hold of his brain with claws of sheer horror.

*He said the nixie could look like anything it wants,* his mind raced. *What if the real Sadie was already dead by the time I woke up to save her?*

Sadie saw the expression on Cory's face and blanched. "What—what are you thinking?" she asked, sounding a bit defensive. "I just don't think you should be wandering around out there after dark. If my grandfather is right, this nixie thing might get you."

Cory felt his mouth grow dry as he tried to answer. *That makes sense,* he thought, trying to stay calm. *No, it doesn't,* he scolded himself. *Her grandfather is just trying to scare us with that crazy story. Well, she may have fallen for it, but I'm out of here.* "Uh, my family," Cory said weakly. "I've got to get back to my mom, dad, and sisters."

*Could Sadie be a nixie?*

*Could her grandfather?*

*Could Cory?*

sacrifice: an offering to a god

Sadie opened her mouth to answer when something thudded—or did it splash?—against the door of the small cabin. With a scream, she jumped away. "Look!" she whispered. She held one hand over her mouth and pointed with the other at the bottom of the door.

There was another splashy thud, harder than before, and the wood of the door frame creaked in response. Cory slowly turned to see what Sadie was pointing at and saw a growing stain of water spread through the crack under the door . . . as if something very big and wet were standing on the other side.

Feeling his control begin to slip, Cory unglued his eyes from the horrible stain and stared at Sadie's grandfather, then at Sadie. They were both trembling, and in a flash of terror Cory knew he had made a mistake. Sadie wasn't the nixie, after all, and if her grandfather was right, the *real* nixie was behind that door!

Another wet thud threatened to break down the thin barrier between Cory and the wet being that was outside, a wet being that was probably a nixie who was very angry with *him*.

# The Monster of Lake Champlain

**Real-life settings often inspire imaginary tales of terror.**

On July 5, 1977, a woman by the name of Sandra Mansi took a most unusual snapshot. She reportedly saw a commotion in the otherwise peaceful waters of Lake Champlain, a huge body of water that stretches along the northern border between the states of New York and Vermont. The disturbance began with a rippling that Mansi first thought to be caused by a school of fish. Then, to her surprise, something began to rise from the water. It was the head and long, slender neck of some sort of animal. Stunned, the woman managed to focus and shoot the snapshot before the creature vanished.

Mansi didn't report the incident immediately, fearing that people might think she was crazy. But eventually, since others also had claimed to see the extraordinary animal, she informed the authorities and turned over the photograph for close <u>scrutiny</u>. The experts who inspected the picture seemed to feel that it was <u>authentic</u>, but no one could identify the creature. Since that time, the original photo and the negative have been lost.

The first written record of the beast, who is known as Champ, was made in 1609 by the man the lake was named

scrutiny: examination

authentic: real; true

for, French explorer Samuel de Champlain. He described it as a 20-foot-long snakelike creature with a horse-shaped head. In August of 1878, six people on a pleasure cruise of the lake sighted Champ, or one of its <u>descendants</u>, again. The witnesses claimed they had seen a beast about 50 feet long, with a long neck and two folds at the back of its head, swimming smoothly through the water. They also added that it appeared to have three humps on its back. Since then there have been dozens of similar reports.

---

**In the 1800s, circus showman P. T. Barnum offered a $50,000 reward to anyone who could provide positive proof of the creature's existence.**

---

Is there an undiscovered life-form in the cold, deep body of water? Lake Champlain is 100 miles long and 13 miles across at its widest point. Its deepest point measures some 400 feet. Certainly something might inhabit this humongous lake and manage to remain hidden, despite <u>exhaustive</u> search efforts. In the 1800s, circus showman P. T. Barnum offered a $50,000 reward to anyone who could provide positive proof of the creature's existence. The reward was never collected.

descendants: children and grandchildren

exhaustive: thorough

## LAKE MONSTERS OF THE WORLD

Champ isn't the only frightful monster reportedly seen in the world's deep, cold lakes. Here is a list of a few of the others.

| MONSTER | LOCATION |
|---------|----------|
| Manipogo | Lake Manitoba, Canada |
| Ogopogo | Okanagan Lake, British Columbia, Canada |
| Silver Lake Monster | Silver Lake, New York |
| Slimey Slim | Lake Payette, Idaho |
| Gloucester Monster | Gloucester Harbor, Massachusetts |
| Flathead Lake Monster | Flathead Lake, Montana |
| Morag | Loch Morar, Scotland |
| Loch Ness Monster | Loch Ness, Scotland |
| The Great Lake Monster | Storsjon, Sweden |

# The Good Deed

## ▼ Learning from the Story

A good story will help you to see the setting, to imagine that you're standing right there. Work with several other students to draw a picture of one of the settings in "The Good Deed." You might illustrate one of these places.

- the campsite
- Cory's cove
- the cabin

Use details from the story and your own imagination to fill in any holes. Now compare your sketch with those of other groups. Are they the same? Are they different? Notice that other groups put some of their own experiences into their sketches.

## ▼ Putting It into Practice

Think about your own travel story.

Where is it going to take place?
What will the setting look like?

For most of your stories, the setting will play an important part. Once you have a mental image of the setting, make a more concrete image of it.

Create a setting collage. Glue together magazine photos, color copies, and colored paper to create the setting you have in mind. Don't be afraid to eliminate things that don't belong in the photos and to add things that do.

# Just Deserts

Some people never seem to get what they deserve. **Or do they?**

Slowly Evan's thoughts crawled back into his head. He tried to open his eyes, but for some reason, the lid of his right eye seemed to be stuck. And his right shoulder hurt, too—*really* hurt. As his awareness grew, he realized he was curled into a ball and wedged against something hard, yet soft at the same time.

*Where am I?* he wondered.

It was silent—somehow *too* silent. Forcing his right eye open with his fingertips, Evan saw that he was inside the cabin of a small plane, the front nose of which was buried in the ground. The Plexiglas window was cracked all the way across, but was still in its frame.

"I've been in a plane crash," Evan whispered in awe, blinking to clear his blurry vision. He peered outside through a tiny window of the wreckage. *Where am I?* he wondered, looking at what appeared to be nothing but a vast desert.

As his eyes refocused, Evan saw that the plane rested on a slant, tilting to the pilot's side—and the pilot was <u>grotesquely</u> wrapped around the steering wheel.

**grotesquely:** in a strangely twisted way

"Dad!" he cried, as things suddenly started coming back to him. "Are you—" But he didn't have to finish his sentence. He could see that his father was dead.

Falling back in shock, Evan's face erupted into tears. Then he realized that he was leaning against the back of the passenger seat. *Where was his mother?* his mind raced. *Had she been in the plane, too?* With another sickening rush of memory, Evan could hear her scolding his dad for not wearing his seat belt. And then he knew for certain that, yes, she too had been with them.

Wrenching himself free of the strap around his waist, Evan squirmed between the two front seats, wincing at the pain from his near-useless right shoulder. He gasped when he saw his mother's body. She was slumped over, with only her seat belt holding her in place. He could see now that her seat had come loose and had slid forward—whether from the impact of the crash or due to Evan's seat slamming into it, he couldn't say. But the question now was, was she alive?

Coming to grips with the horror of what he was seeing, Evan bent down and examined his mother. "Mom?" he croaked, patting her gently.

She was still breathing, but she didn't respond.

"Mom!" he said louder. "Can you hear me?"

When he still got no response, Evan leaned across his mother and pushed at the door handle. But this effort was too much for him, and his head started to spin, followed by a dull throb that pounded in his right temple. Afraid he might faint, he sat back for a moment to think.

The frame of the plane was clearly warped and had caused the door to bend out of alignment. He needed to be where his mother was in order to push with all his force on the stuck door. Resolving to tackle the task at hand, he wiped away his tears, then carefully worked his mother free of her belt and laid her as gently as he could to one side. Then he propped himself on her seat and hammered at the door with his feet. With a screech of protest, the door finally wrenched open, and Evan slid out of the plane.

Standing on the dusty, <u>parched</u> floor of a shallow <u>gully</u>, Evan nearly fainted, his vision spinning crazily. He staggered over to the side of the plane, then sank to the ground, his head in his hands. "What the . . . ?" he murmured, feeling something sticky in his hair. He looked at his hand and saw that it was covered with blood. It was the final straw for Evan's already battered mind, and he fainted.

**PREDICT**

*What's going to happen to Evan?*

✳ ✳ ✳

Some time later—he wasn't sure when—Evan woke up to searing heat. His first thought was that the plane was on fire, and he quickly rolled to one side and peered at the wreckage.

But there was no fire, and Evan soon realized that what he had felt was the desert sun, hot as a raging fire, beating down on him. He had no idea how long he had lain there, but he did remember that he had originally knelt in the shade when he had gotten out of the plane. Now there was no shade at all.

**parched:** completely dry

**gully:** a ditch

**nauseated:** sick to one's stomach

Feeling slightly <u>nauseated</u>, Evan lurched to his feet and staggered over to the plane to see if his mom had regained consciousness. She was still lying in the same position he had left her in . . . but was no longer breathing.

"No!" Evan screamed, falling over his mother's lifeless body. In horror, he realized that he was suddenly without parents, without help . . . and totally alone.

That had been yesterday. Now it was morning and he sat in the backseat of the wrecked plane, where he had spent the night. His emotions were gone—baked away by the sun, then frozen during the incredibly cold night. Now he felt nothing—not even sadness at the fact that his parents were dead, not even shock. All he felt was an odd, selfish satisfaction that he alone had survived.

## In horror, he realized that he was suddenly without parents, without help . . . and totally alone.

"Now what?" he asked himself in a hoarse whisper. His shoulder and head still ached. If he moved too quickly, he was sure he would faint. And he was hungry, too—but that was nothing compared to the thirst that seemed to suck the moisture from the walls of his throat.

The way Evan figured it, he had two choices: He could try to find help, or he could wait for help to come to him. Slowly he bent forward and studied the instrument panel. It was smashed beyond use, so he wouldn't be able to radio for help. And he had no idea how long it would take for someone to realize the plane was missing. *It could be hours before they find me,* he thought, beginning to panic. *Or days!*

On the other hand, the idea of crossing the arid landscape, which stretched as far as he could see, was a terrifying one. He could walk in the direction the plane had been headed, but he had no idea how far it was to civilization. It could be close by, or it could be unreachable.

"I don't want to die," he whimpered, feeling a tear roll down his cheek. Then he burst out into hysterical laughter. He hadn't thought there was even that much water left in his body.

Needing to do something to keep his mind off his situation, Evan searched the interior of the plane. He didn't know what he might find in the way of emergency supplies, but he remembered enough to know that his dad, a very methodical man, would have been prepared for any situation. There had to be something in the plane that could help him—there just *had* to be.

In a compartment behind his seat, Evan found a small canvas bag. Feeling hopeful for the first time, he yanked it out of the storage space and unzipped it to find a first aid kit, a flare gun, matches, a few cans of food, and some shiny foil packages marked "Emergency Water."

"I knew you wouldn't let me down, Dad," Evan exclaimed as he tore open one of the packages and gulped down the warm, metallic-tasting liquid. Then he eagerly opened one of the cans only to find hard, dry biscuits. Shrugging, he stuffed a few into his mouth. Although they were tasteless, they sure were better than nothing.

Feeling slightly energized, Evan contemplated his meager rations. There were four more packets of water and two more cans of biscuits. The first aid kit was all but

**arid:** dry

**methodical:** careful; well-organized

**contemplated:** thought about for a long time

**meager:** poor; skimpy

useless to him, since he couldn't see his head wound anyway, and his shoulder couldn't be helped by bandaging. The flare gun would surely be useful if he could figure out how it worked, and the matches might be handy if he actually found some wood to light a fire.

*Stay or go?* he asked himself, sitting in the warming interior of the plane as the day grew hotter and hotter.

In the end, it was the heat that made the decision for him. It had increased so rapidly that he figured he'd fry to death if he stayed inside the plane. So, grabbing the canvas bag, Evan eased himself past the stiff forms of his parents, trying not to look at them, and dropped to the ground outside. He knew it was madness to start walking during the daylight hours, so he dug into the cool, sandy soil in the shadow of the plane and waited for the sun to set.

Dozing on and off throughout the blistering-hot day, Evan woke only long enough to move out of the sunlight when it crept around the body of the plane to shine on him. Then he had to fight with himself not to drink too much from the water packets, giving in only when his throat was so dry he could hardly swallow.

Later that day, as the sun set, Evan began to get ready to set out. *There's nothing to be afraid of,* he told himself over and over again. *There can't be any big animals out there. What would they survive on?*

Finishing a half-full packet of water and glancing back one last time at the wreckage that contained his parents, Evan set off into the longest night of his life.

*Would this story work as well in a different setting? Why or why not?*

Although he thought he was well rested, Evan's strength seemed to fade rapidly as he plodded along. The sky was clear and the moon was bright, but he still managed to stumble over unseen rocks and low, thorny bushes. His head pounding and his shoulder throbbing, Evan felt searing pain with each step he took. And when he stopped, the cold desert air started him shivering. The only good note was that, when he could no longer make his legs move, he sank to the ground and was so exhausted that he instantly fell asleep.

But the blinding sun woke him up in what seemed like minutes. Opening his bleary eyes, Evan stared in dismay at the miles of sand that surrounded him without a break.

*I've got to get out of this heat,* he reasoned, shading his eyes and studying the flat, parched land. Dejected, he sank back to the ground and opened a can of the horribly dry biscuits. He munched on one between sips from his precious package of water and considered his position. The only promise of shelter lay ahead of him, where it looked like there was some sort of dip in the ground. He thought he could see the shape of a large tree there that he could rest under. Pushing himself to move on before the heat of the day set in, Evan started walking.

His vision was a bit better this morning, and soon he was close enough to see that he was approaching another dried-out wash like the one the plane had crashed into. He also saw something else, something that chilled him to the bone despite the unrelenting heat of the morning sun.

There, a little bit before the rim of the gully, was a large path of torn earth that ended at the object he had thought was a tree. Only now he saw what the object truly was—the tail of a plane that lay nose-first in a dry riverbed.

*I can't have come full circle!* he told himself harshly. *It has to be some other plane.*

Breaking into a stumbling run, Evan made his way to the wreck. Before long, he saw what he feared most—it was the same plane, the one that held his dead parents.

Falling to his knees, Evan burst into bitter tears. "The sun set on my right and when I woke up it was on my left," he mumbled to himself like a madman. "I just *couldn't* have walked in a circle. I slept in the same position all night."

But the evidence was there in front of him. He didn't even have to go near the plane to know it was the same one. The smell of death was so thick in the air around the crash, he almost fell over. *I wasted my strength, my rations, on a giant circle!* his mind screamed. *But how?*

Depression settled over him like a <u>shroud</u>, and he sat for a long while, <u>oblivious</u> to his surroundings. Finally Evan made a decision.

"If I can't tell where I'm going at night," he said out loud, "then I'll have to travel by day." And with that, he set off immediately, trying to keep as relaxed a pace as he could. "I'll just take it easy," he told himself, "and I won't push myself too hard." And so, fixing his eyes on a point on the horizon, Evan began walking toward it . . . and walking . . . and walking . . . and walking.

But travel by day was clearly next to impossible. As hard as Evan tried, he couldn't keep his hands off the water. He drained the rest of the open container, and then another full one. Finally he was too exhausted to think

**shroud:** robelike burial garment

**oblivious:** totally unaware of

**PREDICT**

*Do you want to change your prediction? Will Evan ever find help?*

properly and had to stop to rest. Trying to escape the relentless sun, he crawled headfirst into a scraggly bush where he immediately passed out into a deep sleep.

When he woke in the late afternoon, he was pleased to see that the sun was setting directly to his right. "I haven't lost my way *this* time," he congratulated himself, almost giddy with his success.

But his happiness disappeared as soon as he shook out his <u>provisions</u> bag and saw that he was already down to his last packet of water. Trying not to think about what would happen when it was gone, he opened the container and took a sip. Then he got to his feet and started walking.

The sun sank closer to the ground on his right, and as the sky turned violet, an unmistakable shape formed on the horizon. Evan's mouth dropped open, and his brain tried to reject what he was seeing.

It was the tail of a small plane, sticking into the sky at an angle as if it had its nose buried in a ditch. *No,* Evan thought numbly, *this time, it's just not possible!*

Moving almost robotically, his mind teetering on the brink of madness, Evan approached the thing. With each step closer, fear knotted itself more tightly around his heart. Soon he saw the rim of a gully. There, once again, starting a little bit before the rim of the gully, was that same large path of torn earth that ended at the same plane—nose-down in the dirt.

"What's happening to me?" Evan whispered, dropping to his knees. And suddenly an image jumped into his head. It was his dad, fighting to level out the plane. The image was so vivid he could almost hear the

**PREDICT**

*Last chance to change your prediction!*

**provisions:** supply of food and drinks

panic in his parents' voices as the plane dropped to earth.

"I don't understand it," his father was saying in a strained voice. "There must be some kind of leak in the fuel tank. The gauge is on empty."

Evan's mother was silent. Her wide eyes stared from her white face at the ground rushing closer and closer.

"What is *wrong* with me?!" Evan screamed as a final image came into his mind. He and his parents were at the airport, checking out the plane before taking off. Evan hadn't wanted to go on the trip. He'd wanted to stay and go on a camping trip with his friends. But his father had insisted, saying the family didn't spend enough time together. "Now, go check the gas tanks," his father had said sternly, "and quit acting like a spoiled brat."

Evan remembered stomping off, <u>sullenly</u> climbing up on the overhead wing, and yanking off the gas cap. "Fine," he had mumbled, "the tank's full." Then he had slammed the cap back on, not even bothering to give it that <u>crucial</u> turn that would lock it in place.

"Did you make sure to screw the cap on tightly when you replaced it?" his father had asked him when Evan had reported that the tank was full.

Still pouting and feeling mean, Evan had snapped, "Of course I did!"

But now, his guilty conscience would no longer let him lie to the memory of his father. In fact, now Evan realized with dread, his guilty conscience would never let him forget that *he* had caused his parents' death. For his guilt was so strong that it would bring him back to this scene again and again . . . for the rest of his tormented life.

**sullenly:** in a pouting way

**crucial:** vitally important

# Just Deserts

### ▼ Learning from the Story

A good opening paragraph grabs your attention and makes you want to read on. Use the intriguing first paragraph of this story as a story starter. Can you take the story in a completely different direction? Work with several other students and come up with a new story based on this opening paragraph.

### ▼ Putting It into Practice

How effective is the opening paragraph of your disastrous travel story? Work with a group of four or five classmates to get some feedback.

1. Write your opening paragraph on a notecard.
2. Exchange notecards with other members of your group and read each other's opening paragraphs.
3. On the back of each notecard, rate the paragraph on a scale of 1 to 10—1 being "I have to the read the rest of the story NOW!" and 10 being "I'd rather not read it at all." If you can, explain why you felt as you did about the paragraph.

When you get your notecard back, see how well your introduction worked. If most readers gave your opening low marks, get feedback from others on how to improve your paragraph.

# BEYOND THE REEF

ark Ranger Heather Burke picked up the handset. "The Great Barrier <u>Reef</u> stretches more than 1,250 miles along Australia's northern coast," she announced over the intercom as the glass-bottom boat hummed slowly over the spectacular underwater seascape. A few dozen passengers crowded into the glass chamber hanging six feet beneath the square, slow-moving platform. Heather noticed some people in the group wearing T-shirts with the names of colleges in the United States. "For our American visitors," she added, "the reef covers an area equal to about half the size of Texas."

Hank Longley looked with wide-eyed amazement. "It's not just one long plain of coral, is it?" he asked.

The ranger smiled back at Mr. Longley, a stocky, pale man who, after just a few hours in the Australian sun, had acquired a sunburned nose that glowed above his black walrus mustache.

"No, sir," she said. "It's more like a connected group of smaller reefs. There are about 2,500 in all."

Taller and darker than her husband, with salt-and-pepper hair that hung to her shoulders, June Longley

**How can a place so beautiful be so deadly?**

reef: a ridge of rocks or sand near the surface of the water

raised her eyebrows in wonder. "From the air, it looks like it goes on forever," she said.

The Longleys were on vacation with their children Luke, 15, and Cara, 14. They had arrived that morning at a resort in Cairns, a town in North Queensland, Australia. Ahead of them lay two weeks of sun, swimming, and <u>snorkeling</u> in the "eighth wonder of the world." The Longleys had planned—and saved for—the trip for several years. In fact, ever since they'd seen a documentary about the Great Barrier Reef, they'd started what they called a "reef travel fund," putting away every extra penny from birthdays, baby-sitting, tax returns, and bonuses so they could take their dream vacation.

They had snorkeled at home in Connecticut to prepare for diving in the clear turquoise waters that covered the reef. But after the first few minutes of gazing out of the glass across the rainbow <u>spectrum</u> of countless varieties of fish, they knew that diving in the murky waters of Long Island Sound could never have prepared them for the jaw-dropping beauty of what lay before them. Cara Longley pressed her nose against the glass as the boat passed over a stretch of coral that looked like a green, leafy salad.

"Lettuce coral is the name given to the formation we are now passing over," Ranger Burke said, as if reading Cara's mind. "And off to the left is fire coral, which, as its name suggests, can give unsuspecting snorkelers some painful injuries. It's razor sharp."

Luke Longley yawned. This tour was OK, but it wasn't very exciting. Sure, you got to see the reef up close

**snorkeling:** swimming near the surface of the water and breathing through a tube

**spectrum:** a broad range

and personal. And yeah, it was like being in a reverse aquarium. But he wanted to see something else.

*Where are the sharks?* he wondered. *I like coral and angelfish and stuff. But I could see them at Marine World back home. I want to see sharks—big, monstrous man-eaters!*

Track the number of times the author mentions sharks, man-eating sharks!

Luke raised his arms above his head to stretch. He was still tired from the long jet ride halfway around the globe from his home in New England. He had just decided to leave the crowded viewing area to go take a nap when he turned and bumped into someone right behind him. Startled, he found himself face to face with a girl about his age with the most beautiful copper-colored hair and green eyes he'd ever seen.

"G'day," the girl said with a blinding smile and an accent that said she lived here in the Land Down Under.

"Uh . . . sorry," Luke said shyly. "I didn't know anyone was behind me."

"No problem. I didn't mean to crowd you. I just wanted to get a better look at the coral. I can't believe this reef is made up of billions of skeletons."

"Huh?" Luke grunted. "What do you mean, *skeletons?*"

"That's what coral is," the girl explained. "Limestone skeletons of living creatures. Incredible, eh?"

Luke nodded in amazement. Not amazement over the coral—he knew what it was—but over the girl. He'd never seen anyone quite so beautiful.

*Don't stand there like a dummy,* he scolded himself. *Ask her what her name is!*

"I'm Rachel," she said, as if reading his mind. She held out her hand. "Rachel Crossdale."

Luke breathed a sigh of relief and took Rachel's soft palm in his. "Luke," he mumbled. "Luke Longley."

"Luke! Did you see the—" Cara had pushed through the crowd to talk to her brother. But she stopped when she saw that he was . . . uh, busy.

Rachel smiled. "Hello. You must be Luke's sister. You look just like him." She extended her hand. "I'm Rachel Crossdale."

Cara smiled back. She wasn't used to kids her age acting so grown-up and formal. She awkwardly shook Rachel's hand. "I'm Cara. Luke's sister." She giggled. "Oh, right. You figured that out already."

Luke caught his sister's eye and gave a slight sideways jerk of his head that said *Get outta here*. But before Cara could take the hint, their mother and father pushed next to them, trying to get closer to the window. Rachel introduced herself, then tugged at the sleeves of a tall, sunburned man and a slim, red-haired woman. Luke could tell right away they were Rachel's parents.

As the Longleys and Crossdales exchanged greetings, Luke noticed that Mr. Crossdale shook hands left-handed, keeping his right hand in his pocket. The adults seemed to hit it off right away, and while they chatted it came out that both families were staying at the Wellington Arms. Luke smiled at Rachel. This was going to be an awesome vacation.

"We're coming to the outer edge of this section of the reef," Ranger Burke's voice came in, breaking through the chatter. "Beyond this point, the Coral Sea drops off hundreds of feet."

Everyone pushed to the window and looked into the dark blue of the deep ocean—everyone except Luke. He couldn't take his eyes off Rachel. Standing behind the crowd pressing against the glass, he watched her auburn hair sway back and forth as she spoke to Cara and pointed at sea creatures that caught her gorgeous green eyes.

"As the reef slopes down, you'll notice a number of creatures," the ranger went on. "There are some spiny sea urchins off to the right, and if you're careful you might spot a moray eel or two. They nest in the area and have a nasty bite. But don't worry. They're really quite timid—unless disturbed."

Luke daydreamed about how he might impress Rachel as his parents and the Crossdales chatted about hometowns and businesses, and Rachel and Cara chattered away. It worried him how Cara was <u>monopolizing</u> Rachel's time. He'd met Rachel first, and now he felt like the odd man out.

Ranger Burke's voice came over the intercom once again. "We'll be heading back momentarily. But before we do, let me call your attention to the large mollusks off to the left. They are giant clams. Some are three feet across and weigh up to a thousand pounds. Notice what happens as the boat's shadow passes over them."

Ooohs and aaahs rose from the crowd. Luke ignored the group and gazed out at the open sea. *Who cares about clams?* he thought bitterly. *I want to see sharks!*

"Look at that!" Rachel exclaimed. "The clams snapped shut. Our shadow made them close."

"Yeah, cool," Cara said. "Maybe we could wave some cocktail sauce to get them to open up again."

**monopolizing:** keeping something entirely to oneself

Rachel chuckled, but Luke just sighed and stared into the dark blue waters. *Girls!* he thought. Then suddenly he squinted into the distance at a dark <u>torpedo</u> shape.

"Hey, look!" he blurted. "Is that a shark out there?"

An anxious buzz rose from the group as all faces looked into the dark waters. Moments later, a gray shark about five feet long with black-tipped fins swam to the window, then banked left and glided along the length of the boat. Its cold eyes and slightly open mouth gave it the look of a <u>demented</u> killer.

Rachel turned away from the window with a look of wide-eyed terror on her face, and Luke edged closer to her. *She sure had a strong reaction to such a small shark,* he thought. *After all, there's no way it can hurt us in here.*

"The shark that just passed the starboard window was a reef shark," the ranger announced, keeping her voice even and calm. "They sometimes come to the reef to feed on the octopuses that live here. That's their main food." She paused as she noticed some looks of concern among the group. "No need to worry for those who plan to snorkel. We are on regular shark patrol. No one is allowed in the water if there's any activity. And all rangers carry shark batons to ward off any unforeseen problems."

As the intercom clicked off, the shark made another pass at the window, its ghostly pale belly skimming along inches from the glass. Rachel drew back as though she had just received an electrical shock.

"Don't like sharks, huh, Rachel?" Luke asked from over her shoulder.

*Why do you think Rachel reacted this way?*

**torpedo:** a large, cigar-shaped explosive

**demented:** crazy; insane

Rachel shook her copper hair as she looked down at the deck. "Can't stand 'em," she said shakily. "It's why we've waited so long to come to the reef for a holiday. I—I have nightmares."

"It's only a small shark," Luke said, trying to sound like an expert and comfort her at the same time.

Rachel looked at Luke and shook her head. He got the uncomfortable feeling that he had somehow put his foot in his mouth. Then she turned to her father a few feet away and tapped him on the shoulder.

"Daddy, Luke just told me that shark we just saw is *only* a small shark," she said sarcastically. "How big was the shark that—" She stopped and looked away from her father, tears welling in her eyes. She was unable to finish her sentence.

Mr. Crossdale turned to face Luke. He held his hands four or five feet apart as though measuring the length of the shark Rachel was referring to. As he spread his arms, Luke's eyes focused on the man's right hand—or what was left of it. Mr. Crossdale had only a thumb and index finger. In the area where his other fingers and palm should have been, there was just empty space. Mr. Crossdale's hand was like a <u>pincer</u> with a plum-colored band of flesh attaching it to his wrist.

"It happened when Rachel was five or six," Mr. Crossdale explained without waiting for Luke to ask. "We were at a beach outside of Sydney."

Just then the boat jerked as its engines reversed and it turned back toward the <u>inlet</u> where it docked. Mr. Crossdale paused and looked out of the glass into the dark ocean as if remembering the incident. Luke saw several more torpedo

**pincer:** a claw, like those of crabs and lobsters

**inlet:** a narrow strip of water extending into the land

shapes in the distance but didn't say anything. Instead, he listened carefully to Mr. Crossdale's story.

"I saw some bloke in a wet suit swimming far out past the surf line—maybe a hundred meters," Mr. Crossdale continued. "Suddenly he began struggling. It looked like he was having trouble keeping his head above water."

As Rachel's father went on with his story, other people in the cramped glass room turned from their underwater sightseeing to listen. Luke saw that Rachel and Mrs. Crossdale had their arms around each other's waists as though the memory was too frightening to recall alone.

"I was closer to the man than the lifeguards were. And I'm a strong swimmer." Mr. Crossdale smiled proudly. "In fact, I used to be a lifeguard in my younger days."

Luke wasn't surprised that Mr. Crossdale had been a lifeguard. The man had the lean, broad-shouldered build of a well-conditioned swimmer. Although Luke was the top freestylist on the Madison High swim team as a freshman, he had the distinct feeling that Mr. Crossdale could swim circles around him—<u>mutilated</u> hand or not.

"Anyway," Mr. Crossdale went on, "I grabbed a board and paddled out as quickly as I could. When I got close I saw why the guy was struggling." Mr. Crossdale paused and ran his left hand through his thinning sandy hair. "He was surrounded by sharks—'only small ones,' as you put it, Luke. They were reef sharks drawn in close to shore by who knows what. Regardless, they had the poor fellow in a real predicament. He grabbed for me, and I saw that the right arm of his wet suit was empty and shredded. I reached into the water to get hold of him, and suddenly a shark rose straight up between us."

**mutilated:** seriously injured by tearing off some part

Rachel let out a half-choked sob and sat down. Mrs. Crossdale looked at her husband with concern. "Do you really think we should tell this story now, John?" she asked.

The hushed attention of the people in the glass room answered her question. Mr. Crossdale *had* to finish the story.

Speaking softly as if remembering the pain, he went on. "Before I could react, I felt a pressure on my hand—a weight yanking it down deeper. My arm was into the water shoulder deep. Then another shark hit me . . . here." Mr. Crossdale pushed up the sleeve of his shirt. At his elbow was a deep, purplish hole. It looked as though the muscles had been torn away from the joint, leaving only the bone and a thin layer of scar tissue.

"There was blood squirting everywhere—like a fountain. Naturally, I went into shock. I looked at my hand and wondered, *Is that my hand?*" Mr. Crossdale laughed and looked at the crowd as if he'd made a joke. "Luckily, the lifeguards were close by in a longboat. They got me and the other fellow back to the beach. He was in bad shape—worse than me. When they unzipped his wet suit his body was in pieces, and he bled to death within half an hour. I was lucky. They flew me to a hospital and patched me up." Mr. Crossdale nodded to his wife and daughter. "My wife and daughter saw everything. They saw what *small* sharks can do."

Cara looked at her parents and shuddered. Luke felt his face burn. The horrible story didn't frighten him as much as it made him feel ignorant. He'd made a fool of himself in front of Rachel—in front of everyone in the boat.

*Boy,* he thought, *my dream vacation is sure getting off to a lousy start!*

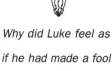

*Why did Luke feel as if he had made a fool of himself?*

A week later, the Crossdales and the Longleys boarded a twin-hulled catamaran piloted by Park Ranger Burke. The petite yet tough-looking young woman whom everyone called Heather piloted the two families about ten miles offshore to a long stretch of reef, not far from the area the group had seen on their first day in Australia.

Luke tightened the diving mask around his head, clamped his teeth around his snorkel's mouthpiece, and slipped into the water lapping against the diving platform of the catamaran. Sighing with pleasure as the sea surrounded him, he floated on his back. They'd gone snorkeling a lot already, and he still couldn't get used to the bathwater warmth of the tropical ocean.

"How's the water, Luke?" Rachel called as Luke's head bobbed above the clear water. "Too cold, I hope. If it is, I've a good excuse *not* to go in."

Luke tried to smile, but the mask pressing down on his face held his cheeks in place. He pushed the mask up on his forehead and stood in the neck-deep water. "Sorry, Rachel, the water's perfect. It's even warmer than the pool back at the hotel."

"But there aren't any sharks in the pool, remember?" Rachel said, offering him a pouting face.

"There aren't any sharks out here, either," Luke countered. He pointed to the ranger, who was anchoring the boat and getting ready to come into the water. "Heather said no sharks have been sighted since that first day on the boat a week ago."

Then Luke pointed to his parents and to Cara

adjusting their masks and snorkels. "Do you think my family would go snorkeling if they thought there were any sharks? Even your parents have been in every day."

But Rachel just shook her head. "Sorry," she called. "It's just not for me."

Luke noticed how seeing the shark that first day had put a damper on all of Rachel's activities since. While he, Cara, and his parents had spent every day exploring the wonders of the reefs with experienced divers like the park ranger, Rachel had shopped or sat by the pool reading. Even Mr. and Mrs. Crossdale had become frustrated by Rachel's reluctance to go into the water. Every day they coaxed her to go with them, then just ended up leaving her at the Wellington and going off with the Longleys. Today was the first day she said she *might* consider giving snorkeling a try. Everyone was just glad that she had decided to come out on the boat.

"Come on, Rachel," Luke pleaded. "I'll keep a special watch for sharks, and I'll let you know if I see even a hint of one."

Finally, after a little more coaxing, Rachel agreed to give it a try. Sliding gingerly into the water, she carefully let herself go under and in two swift strokes was next to Luke. Laughing, she spit out her snorkel and gave him a swift kiss on the cheek.

"You're right," she said. "The water *is* perfect!" She took Luke's hand and pulled him toward deeper water. "Come on! Let's not wait for the others."

"Hey, wait for me!" Cara cried as she saw Luke and

Rachel swimming off. "I don't want to be stuck with the adults!"

"Hold on, you two!" Park Ranger Burke shouted through cupped hands. "The rules are you have to wait for—" She stopped and shook her head.

Luke and Rachel had already sunk beneath the surface, their Day-Glo green snorkels poking above the water as they paddled away.

❋ ❋ ❋

Luke had a hard time keeping up with Rachel. She was a strong swimmer, like her father, and since this was her first day exploring, she was supercharged, gliding through the water as if she had gills. Luke looked back and saw that the rest of the group were so far behind they looked like tiny Day-Glo fish. He wanted to wait—but he wanted to be with Rachel more. Taking a deep breath, he headed out after her.

The water deepened to about fifteen feet as the two teenagers continued toward the outer edge of the reef. Luke followed Rachel as she dove to get a closer look at the darting flashes of silver and gold that were parrot fish, damselfish, surgeonfish, and all kinds of tropical <u>denizens</u>. Colors moved and shapes changed like a kaleidoscope before Luke's unbelieving eyes. There were abalone and anemones, sea cucumbers and urchins. And boy, was there coral—coral of every color in the spectrum!

Luke and Rachel swam farther and farther ahead, unable to contain their joy at the underwater wonders they were seeing, unaware of how long they had been in the

**PREDICT**

*Can you guess what's going to happen to Luke and Rachel?*

**denizens:** occupants; creatures who live there

water or how far ahead of the others they were. Luke felt his heart hammering in his chest, but he wasn't sure if it was from swimming fast or from being alone with Rachel. She pointed to a field of coral off to their right and dove down toward it. Luke followed, his attention captured by the pinkish-orange coral floor.

In two swift strokes, Rachel had almost reached the coral bed. Luke was amazed at how strong she was, and wanted to show that he could move faster underwater than she could. When he was nearly beside her, he kicked his flippers and pulled hard with his arms, trying to reach the coral before she did.

But Luke misjudged both the distance to the coral and his own strength. Before he could stop his descent, he plowed into a protruding edge of the hard, pink, spiny limestone. For all of its delicate beauty, the coral had ridges as sharp as jagged razors. Luke groaned as he felt it tear into the thick meat of his shoulder muscle beside his collarbone.

Rachel turned when she heard Luke grunt through his snorkel. When she saw him suddenly rising to the surface in a cloud of air bubbles, she quickly rose up beside him. As her head popped above the water, she saw Luke wincing in pain.

"Luke! Are you all right?" she cried in a shaky voice. "I saw you hit that ridge of coral. You didn't break anything, did you?"

"Naw. But I sliced up my shoulder a little. Ow!" Luke exclaimed, as he treaded water and rubbed the bloody torn area on his shoulder. "Man, it really burns!"

"It was fire coral. Remember what Heather said the

first day?"

Luke shook his head. "No. I wasn't listening." Luke smiled. "I was looking at you."

Rachel smiled shyly, but her smile faded quickly when Luke pulled his hand away from his shoulder and blood dribbled from his sliced flesh into the water. "You're *bleeding!*" she said, fear creeping into her voice.

"I'm okay. Come on, let's keep going." Luke was doing his best to ignore the stinging cut and the salt water biting into it. He wanted to appear brave to Rachel, but it wasn't easy. His cut really hurt.

"Are you *nuts?*" Rachel asked in disbelief. "Don't you know you're not supposed to swim in the ocean if you're bleeding?"

Luke felt his face redden. He'd been so caught up in being alone with Rachel—and with acting tough—that he'd forgotten about sharks. Blood was a magnet for them. They could sense a drop hundreds of yards away. He looked down and saw a red cloud coloring the turquoise water around his shoulder.

"You're right," Luke said, trying to control a sudden wave of fear rising in him. "We'd better head back." He put his snorkel in his mouth—then stopped.

They looked at each other as the same thought struck them. They'd swum so far so fast, diving every which way, that they'd lost sight of the catamaran. Neither Luke nor Rachel was sure where they were. They looked for the snorkels of the others poking up above the water, but saw nothing but lapping waves. There were several shapes on the flat, turquoise horizon, but neither Rachel nor Luke

could tell which speck was their boat.

Rachel's eyes widened under her mask and Luke knew that if she let fear beat her, they'd both be in trouble. He willed himself to remain calm.

"We have to swim away from the darker water," he said, gesturing in the direction of dark blue water. "We know that's where the reef ends."

Rachel nodded and smiled uncertainly. "They're probably looking for us right now," she said. "I'll bet my mom and dad are upset."

Luke nodded. "My folks are probably ticked off, too. Let's get going."

The two worried snorkelers began to swim back toward a speck that they thought might be the catamaran, making certain that the dark blue of deeper water was always on the same side—their left. Luke's shoulder pounded with pain as he plowed through the warm water, unable to keep up with Rachel, who remained a few lengths ahead. Nervously, Luke looked back every few minutes to make sure that sharks were not tracking the bloody trail he was leaving behind.

Suddenly Luke felt a tap on his right side. Startled, he glanced over and was relieved to see Rachel, who had slowed and was smiling as she pointed off to her right. Far in the distance were the tiny silhouettes of what appeared to be several adults. She squeezed Luke's hand softly, and for a moment he forgot the dull ache in his shoulder.

But his relief didn't last long. Seconds later, Rachel's grip tightened and Luke heard a muffled scream coming through her snorkel. She let go of his hand and pointed

**PREDICT**

*Will Luke and Rachel get back alive? What makes you think as you do?*

frantically—no longer to her right, but to her left. Those shapes in the water that they had thought were human— they were torpedo shapes!

In horror, Luke saw a dark, wiggling mass of sharks moving from the deep water toward the reef, growing larger right before his eyes. *That's odd,* Luke said to himself, his numbed brain still managing to think. *The sharks can't be following my trail because they're coming at us from the side, not coming from behind.*

Fighting a new wave of panic, Luke squeezed Rachel's hand. Then he motioned for her to go on in the direction they thought the boat was in. As soon as the sharks caught the scent of his blood, they'd surely go after him, and maybe Rachel would make it to the boat.

> In horror, Luke saw a dark, wiggling mass of sharks moving from the deep water toward the reef . . .

But Rachel's fear was so powerful she began to shake her head back and forth hysterically, clutching Luke's good shoulder as though she were drowning. Determined to remain strong, Luke popped his head above the surface, grabbed Rachel by both shoulders, and forced her head above the water. Then he spit the snorkel from his mouth and shouted, "Get a grip, Rachel! You're a strong swimmer.

Lead the way back. I'll follow at a distance. If the sharks get too close, I'll swim in a different direction while you bring help!"

Rachel shook her head, then spit out her mouthpiece and shouted, "No! No! I can't make it! The sharks will—" But her voice cut off as it rose into a shriek.

Luke shook her hard, paddling with his flippers to keep his head above water. "Listen to me, Rachel! You don't have a choice!" He grabbed the mouthpiece of her snorkel and pushed it gently back into her mouth. Then he shoved her as hard as he could away from the oncoming school of sharks and in what he hoped was the direction of the boat.

Back underwater, Luke fell behind Rachel as she cut through the water with powerful thrusts of her flippers. He tried to keep up, but his throbbing shoulder and the long swim had weakened him. By now he could see that the sharks were about the size of the reef shark he had seen on the first day. They were coming nearer and nearer, but they didn't seem to be in any kind of attack mode. In fact, it looked like the sharks were fleeing from something attacking *them*.

For a moment Luke pondered this. The only thing they would be swimming from was . . . something *bigger!*

At the very same instant that this terrible realization hit him, Luke saw the silhouette looming behind the school of sharks. It looked at least two or three times bigger than the prey it swam after. In fact, it looked like a giant bomber among tiny planes. Through the clear water and the shrinking distance, Luke saw dark stripes on the

flank of the huge creature. Then, as it cut its way through the school of smaller sharks, he saw the blunt snout and sharp, pointed tail.

*Tiger shark!* Luke's mind screamed. He'd read about the ferocious man-eaters before the trip. They lived in shallow tropical waters and sometimes grew to be twelve feet in length or more . . . and they ate anything in their path. Luke's heart pounded as he recalled the picture he'd seen of the stomach contents taken from a dead tiger shark. Laid out on a dock were a coil of copper wire, a wallet, a dog's paw, and several wine bottles!

Luke had begun his vacation wishing to see a large shark, but now that he knew his wish was coming true he'd have given anything to see those boring tropical fish he'd scoffed at before. Hardly able to breathe, his fear rising in his throat, Luke watched as Rachel extended the distance between them. As far as he knew, she had not seen the tiger shark. He hoped she wouldn't. He hoped that she—

Suddenly Luke saw billowing clouds of blood. The tiger shark was slashing through the smaller sharks, ripping them to pieces. As the large shark <u>dismembered</u> the smaller ones, its prey also went mad with the smell of blood in the water . . . and a killing frenzy began.

As Luke watched in horror, hoping that he wouldn't become part of their meal, he saw that Rachel was far enough ahead to escape the slaughter. *His* fate, however, was not so certain. It was only a matter of time before the tangle of frantic and dying sharks would <u>engulf</u> him. He gulped a lungful of air and dove to the bottom. In swimming class

**dismembered:** cut or tore the limbs from

**engulf:** to swallow up

*What would you do if you were Luke?*

he'd held his breath for over three minutes once. Now he'd probably have to hold it longer—his life depended on it.

*If I can just stay perfectly still below them and remain unnoticed*, he thought, *they're busy enough killing themselves to pass right over me.*

Crouching on the bottom, holding onto a ridge of coral to keep his buoyant body from rising, Luke watched in disbelief as a dozen small sharks shot over him like speeding missiles. Then his eyes widened in awe as the huge tiger shark swam by only six or seven feet over his head, the intestines of smaller sharks trailing from its jaws.

As the ominous shadow passed across his body, Luke knew this was his chance. But as he tried to rise from the coral bed, he felt a heavy weight holding him back. He couldn't move. Panicked, Luke looked down at his foot. A huge clam, its instincts triggered by the shadow of the giant shark, had closed tightly around his left ankle.

Frantic, Luke tried to slip his foot out of his flipper, but the thousand-pound mollusk had a firm grip. *This is it!* Luke's mind shrieked. *I'm going to die!*

As he fought against the pull of the clam, Luke felt his lungs about to burst. Then, suddenly he saw the tiger shark turn and whirl its monstrous body down toward him. In his oxygen-starved brain, he slowly realized that his frantic movements had caught the beast's attention. Nothing more than a helpless spectator to his own death, Luke watched as the green striped body zeroed in. Then, just before the creature slammed into him, he closed his eyes.

Instantly, the sound of cracking bone and tearing flesh

echoed in Luke's head as he screamed. Then bloody bubbles rose to the surface . . . and Luke was rising with them.

Through the red plume trailing behind him like a rocket's exhaust, Luke saw sharks below surround the giant clam. They were all fighting for the morsel that dangled from its giant shell—it was a leg. Luke wondered whose it was. Then he saw blood jetting into the empty space below his knee. The last thing he saw before blackness swallowed him was a strange hand reaching out to him—a hand with just a thumb and an index finger.

✳ ✳ ✳

*"Luke! Luke!"*

Through the haze of pain, Luke heard Cara's voice. Then he heard the sound of a helicopter. When he opened his eyes, his father and Mr. Crossdale were holding a <u>tourniquet</u> around the remains of his left leg. A paramedic readied an injection for the pain he knew he should be feeling, but Luke felt nothing except Rachel's tears splashing onto his face as she cradled his head.

"I couldn't—I couldn't move," he said, gritting his teeth. "I was trapped."

Rachel looked back beyond the reef. "Killers! Nothing but bloody killers!" she screamed.

"Killers." Luke whispered the word and closed his eyes as the injection did its work. Someday he'd have to tell Rachel how a killer had saved his life . . . from a giant clam.

**tourniquet:** a device to stop bleeding

# The East Coast of
# AUSTRALIA

**Horror stories like "Beyond the Reef"
are often inspired by real-life horrors, like these
monsters of the deep.**

The two honeymooners were <u>scuba diving</u> in Byron Bay, a popular beach area 370 miles north of Sydney, the capital of the Australian state of New South Wales. Married less than three weeks, Debbie and John Ford swam in beautiful clear water at a depth of about forty feet on June 9, 1993.

Suddenly John saw a huge, menacing shadow gliding beneath the surface of the water and heading toward his wife. John knew his wife was in great danger, so he swam between her and the advancing creature. Seconds later a sixteen-foot great white shark grabbed John in its huge jaws and began shaking him violently before taking him below the surface to his death. Debbie's life, however, had been spared.

Only four days earlier a thirty-four-year-old woman was attacked in another area off the east coast of Australia and carried away by a twelve-foot great white shark. The attack was witnessed by her husband and five young children. The only remains consisted of a <u>severed</u> human leg with a diving fin still attached.

**scuba diving:** swimming underwater using oxygen tanks

**severed:** cut-off

The east coast of Australia has had more shark attacks and fatalities than any part of the world, yet compared to other causes of death—like traffic accidents or disease—the risk to swimmers and scuba divers is still minimal. Keep repeating that over and over again while you're splashing around in the waters off eastern Australian beaches!

. . . "worldwide there are probably fifty to seventy-five shark attacks annually, resulting in about five to ten deaths."

George Burgess, director of the International Shark Attack File, which keeps records of all reported shark attacks, wrote that "worldwide there are probably fifty to seventy-five shark attacks annually, resulting in about five to ten deaths." He declared that "many more people are injured and killed on land while driving to and from the beach than by sharks in the water."

The risk may be minimal, but that doesn't make the prospect of a shark attack any less unnerving. Great white sharks can grow to twenty-five or more feet in length and weigh several thousand pounds. Their terrifying mouths, lined from front to back with razor-sharp teeth, are huge enough to swallow a person whole. These sharks are

eating machines and will devour almost anything, including each other.

If the hairs on your neck aren't standing straight up from the very possibility of a shark attack, keep your eyes peeled for the beautiful but <u>lethal</u> Australian sea wasp, the most venomous jellyfish in the world. There are signs on certain eastern Australian beaches that read, "Warning—Sea Wasps Are Deadly in These Waters Between October and May."

Brush up against the transparent tentacles of the sea wasp and you'll experience terrible pain, partial paralysis, massive welts on the skin, and possible death within a few minutes. This lovely little creature has caused the death of sixty-six people off Queensland since 1880. Numerous others have survived the <u>ordeal</u>, often with lasting scars and very bad memories.

Regardless of the risks that may exist, more people than ever flock to the picturesque beaches of Australia's eastern coast for a day of fun in the sun and surf. After all, the odds are definitely in their favor.

Care to take a dip?

**lethal:** deadly

**ordeal:** test or experience

## ▼ Learning from the Story

See how the author weaves details throughout "Beyond the Reef." Work in groups of three–four classmates.

1. Each group member needs a different-colored pad of sticky notes.
2. Have each person select a different type of detail, such as a detail about Luke, Rachel, the setting, or sharks.
3. Read the story aloud. When one of your details is mentioned, put one of your sticky notes on the chalkboard or a flip chart. After the story is finished, tally the results to see how many times your specific type of detail was woven into the story.

## ▼ Putting It into Practice

Read over your own disastrous travel story. Are there key events at the end of the story that could be casually hinted at in the beginning? For example, early in the story you might mention a barking dog that woke you up in the night—hinting at the wild dogs that torment you later in the story. Weave in important details and cut out unimportant ones.

# RESTING DEEP

**Not all visits with grandparents are boring!**

My parents dropped me off at his house late last night.

Greaty's house.

That's what I call him, "Greaty"—short for Great-grandpa. He's the oldest in the family. He's buried two wives, two sons, and one daughter.

His house is small: a living room, a bedroom, and a tiny kitchen. It's really a shack in a row of other shacks, where ancient people cling to their last days.

It smells old here. It smells salty, like the sea. And Greaty's always eating the fish he catches.

"Good to see you, Tommy," he said to me at the door, smiling his long-toothed smile.

Whenever I see his smile, I run my tongue along my braces, feeling the crooked contour of my own teeth, wondering if one day mine will look like his, all yellow and twisted.

"Ready for a good day of fishing tomorrow?" he asked.

"Sure, I guess."

My parents left me here to spend a night and a day. They do this every year, four times a year. It started when

I was little. It had to do with my fear of water. Mom and Dad decided that the best way for me to get over it was to send me out with Greaty on his big fishing boat. Then I'd see how much fun water could be.

But it didn't work that way.

Greaty would always tell tales of sharks and whales and mermaids who dragged fishermen down to their watery graves. Going out with him made me more afraid of the water than I had been before, so afraid that I never learned to swim. Still, I went out with him and continue to go. It's become a family tradition. Sometimes, I'm ashamed to say, I hope for the day when Greaty joins his two wives, two sons, and one daughter, so I don't have to go out to sea with him ever again.

❊ ❊ ❊

It is an hour before dawn now. Greaty and I always set out when everything is cold, dark, and still, and my veins feel full of ice water. I watch him as he prepares his boat. It's an old fishing boat, its wooden hull marred with gouges from years of banging up against the dock. When a wave rides it high against its berth, I can see the <u>barnacles</u> crusted on its belly. It has been years since Greaty has bothered to have them scraped off.

He calls his boat the *Mariana*, "named after the deepest <u>trench</u> in the ocean," he once told me. "That trench is seven miles deep, and it's where the great mysteries of the world still lie undiscovered."

I sometimes think about the trench. I think about all the ships and planes that have fallen down there in wars.

**barnacles:** shelled animals that attach themselves permanently to rocks, ships, or whales

**trench:** a deep ditch

I imagine being in a ship that had seven miles to sink before hitting bottom. That's like falling from space.

We set out, and by the time dawn arrives, we are already far from shore. I can tell that the day is not going to be a pleasant one. The sun is hidden behind clouds. There is a storm to the north, and it's churning up the waves.

Greaty heads due north into the choppy waves. He stares at the horizon and occasionally says something to me just to let me know he hasn't forgotten me.

"Today's going to be an exceptional day," he tells me. "One day in a million. I can feel it in my bones."

I can feel it in my bones, too, but not what Greaty feels. I feel a miserable sense of dread creaking through all of my joints. Something is going to happen today—I know it, and it is not something good. I imagine giant tidal waves looming over us, swallowing us in cold waters and sending us down to the very bottom, where it is so dark the fish don't have eyes.

＊ ＊ ＊

Half an hour later, the shore behind us is just a thin line of gray on the horizon. Greaty has never taken me out this far before. Never.

"Maybe we'd better stop here," I tell him. "We're getting kind of far from shore."

"We'll stop soon," he says. "We're almost there."

*Almost where?* I wonder. But Greaty doesn't say anything more about it. His silence is strange. I don't know what he's thinking—I never do.

*How does the author set you up to expect disaster?*

And then something suddenly strikes me in a way that it has never struck me before—I don't know my great-grandfather. I've spent days and weekends with him every few months for my entire life, but I don't *know* him. I don't know what he thinks and what he feels. All I know about him is the way he baits his hooks, the way he talks about fishing. I can't get the feeling out of my head that suddenly I'm out on a boat with a stranger.

"You know how many great-grandchildren I have, Tommy?" he asks, shoving a wad of chewing tobacco into the corner of his mouth. "Twelve."

"That's a lot," I say with a nervous chuckle.

"You know how many of them I take fishing with me?" He stares at me, chewing up and down, with a smile on his crooked, tobacco-filled mouth.

"Just me?"

He points his gnarled, bony finger at me.

"Just you."

He waits for me to ask the obvious question, but I don't.

"You want to know why I take only you?" he asks. "Well, I'll tell you. There's your cousins, the Sloats. With all the money they've got, they can buy their kids anything in the world. Those kids are set for life. Then there's your other cousins, the Tinkertons. They've got brains coming out of them like sweat. They'll all amount to something. And your Aunt Rebecca's kids—they're beautiful. All that golden hair—they'll get by on their looks."

"So?" I ask.

"So," he says. "What about you?"

*What about me?* I take after my mother—skinny as a rail, a bit of an overbite. And I got my father's big ears, too. OK, so I'm not the best-looking kid. As for money, we live in a small, crummy house, and we probably won't ever afford anything better. As for brains, I'm a C student. Always have been.

The old man sees me mulling myself over. "Now do you know?" he asks.

I can't look at Greaty. I can only look down, feeling inadequate and ashamed. "Because I'm ugly . . . because I'm poor . . . because I'm stupid?"

Greaty laughs at that, showing his big teeth. I never realized how far the gums had <u>receded</u> away from them, like a wave recedes from the shore. He should have had all his teeth pulled out and replaced by fake ones. The way they are now, they're awful, like teeth in a skull.

"I picked you because you were the special one, Tommy," he says. "You were the one *without* all the things the others have. To me that makes you special."

He turns the wheel and heads toward the dark storm clouds on the horizon.

"I was like you, Tommy," he tells me. "So you're the one I want to take with me."

＊ ＊ ＊

The waves begin to get rough, rolling up and down like tall black hills and deep, dark valleys. The wind breathes past us, moaning like a living thing, and I feel seasickness begin to take hold in my gut.

Greaty must see me starting to turn green.

*What does Greaty mean when he says "take with me"?*

**receded:** moved back or away from

"How afraid of the water are you, Tommy?" he asks.

"About as afraid as a person can get," I tell him.

"You know," he says, "the ocean's not a bad place. When I die, I would like to die in the ocean." He paused. "I think I will."

I swallow hard. I don't like it when Greaty talks about dying. He does it every once in a while. It's like he sees the world around him changing—the neighborhood being torn down to build condos, the marshes paved over for supermarkets. He knows that he'll be torn off this world soon, too, so he talks about it, as if talking about it will make it easier when the time comes.

"Why are we heading into the storm?" I ask Greaty.

He doesn't say anything for a long time.

"Don't you worry about that," he finally says coldly. "A man can catch his best fish on the edge of a storm."

We travel twenty minutes more, and as we go I peer over the side, where I see fins—<u>dorsal</u> fins, sticking out of the water—and I'm terrified.

"Dolphins," says Greaty, as if reading the fear in my face.

Sure enough, he is right. Dolphins are riding along with the boat. As I look into the distance, I see dozens of them, all running in line with us, as if it is a race. And then suddenly they stop.

I go to the <u>stern</u> of the boat and look behind us. The dolphins are still there, but they wait far behind. The bottle-tips of their noses poke out of the water, forming a line a hundred yards away, like a barrier marking off one part of the ocean from the other.

**dorsal:** located on or near the back

**stern:** the back of a boat

I look down at the waters we've come into and could swear that, as black as the waters were before, they're even blacker now. And the smell of the sea has changed, too.

Greaty stops the boat.

"We're here," he tells me.

He gets out his fishing rod, and one for me. Then he pulls out bait, <u>impaling</u> the small feeder fish onto tiny barbed hooks.

Suddenly, the boat <u>pitches</u> with a wave. It goes up and down like an elevator—like a wild ride at an amusement park. My stomach hangs in midair and then falls down to my toes.

The water rises around the boat, almost flowing in, but the boat rises with it.

"You know why a boat floats?" he asks me.

"Why does a boat float, Greaty?"

"Because it's too afraid of what's under the water," he says, completely serious.

Greaty throws his line in, and we wait, he sitting there calmly, and I, shivering, with sweaty palms. I watch lightning strike in the far, far distance.

*Greaty knows what he's doing,* I tell myself. *He's been fishing his whole life. He knows how close you can get to a storm and still be safe . . . doesn't he?*

I haven't thrown my line in yet. It's as if throwing a line into the water brings me closer to it, and I don't want to be closer to it. I watch my feeder fish, sewed onto the steel hook, writhe in silent agony until it finally goes limp. Greaty watches the fish die.

**impaling:** stabbing or piercing with something sharp and pointed

**pitches:** plunges up and down

"Dying is the natural course of things, you know," he says. "Bad thing about dying, though, is having to die alone. I don't want to die alone." Then he turns to me and says, "When I go, I want somebody to come with me."

He takes my line, casts it into the water, and hands me back the rod. I feel the line being pulled away from the boat as the hook sinks deeper and deeper. Lightning flashes on the distant horizon.

"The person who dies with me, though, ought to be someone I care about. Someone *special*," he says.

"I gotta use the bathroom," I tell him, even though I don't have to. I just have to get away, as far away as I can. I have to go where I don't see the ocean, or the storm, or Greaty.

I go down to the cabin, and there I feel something cold on my feet. I look down and see water.

I race back up top. "Greaty," I say. "There's water down below! We're leaking."

But he isn't bothered. He just holds his line and chews his tobacco. "Guess old *Mariana* decided she's not so afraid of the ocean after all."

"We gotta start bailing! We have to do something!"

"Don't you worry, Tommy," he tells me in a soft, calm voice. "She takes on a little water now and then. It doesn't mean anything."

"Are you sure?"

"Of course I'm sure."

Then Greaty's line goes taut, and his pole begins to bend. He skillfully fights the fish on the other end, letting out some line, then pulling some in—out, in, out, in, until the fish on the other end is exhausted.

**PREDICT**

*What more could possibly go wrong?*

In the distance behind us, the dolphins watch.

I hear the snagged fish thump against the boat, and Greaty, his old muscles straining, reels it in.

At first I'm not sure what I'm seeing, and then it becomes clear. The thing on the end of the line is like no fish I've ever laid eyes on. It is ugly and gray, covered with slime rather than scales. It has a long neck like a baby giraffe, and its head is filled with teeth. It has only one eye, in the center of its forehead—a clouded, unseeing eye.

Greaty drops the thing onto the deck, and it flops around, making an awful growling, hissing noise. Its head flies to the left and then to the right on the end of its long neck, until finally it collapses.

Greaty looks at it long and hard. Far behind us, the dolphins wait at the edge of the black waters.

"What is it, Greaty?"

"It doesn't have a name, Tommy," he tells me, as he heads into his tackle room. "It doesn't have a name."

He comes out of the boat with a new fishing rod—a heavy pole, with heavy line and a hook the size of a meat hook. He digs the hook into the thing he caught and hurls it back into the ocean, letting it pull out far into the dark waters.

What could he possibly be trying to catch with something that large?

"Greaty, I want to go home now." I can hear the distant rumble of thunder. The storm coming toward us is as black as the sea. When I look down into the cabin, the water level has risen. There is at least a foot of water down there, and the boat is leaning horribly to <u>starboard</u>.

starboard: the right side of a boat

"Greaty!" I scream. "Are you listening to me?"

"We're not going home, Tommy."

I hear what he's saying, but I can't believe it. "What?" I shout at him. "What did you say?"

"Don't you see, Tommy?" he tells me. "There are places out here—wondrous places that no one has ever charted. Places deeper than the Mariana Trench, bottomless places where creatures dwell that no man has ever seen."

The boat pitches terribly. Water pours in from the side.

"We're going to be part of that mystery, Tommy, you and me, together. We're going to rest deep."

"No!" I scream. "You can't do this! I don't want to die out here!"

"Tommy, you're not doing anyone else on this earth any good," he explains to me. "You won't be missed by many, and even then you won't be missed for long. I'm the only one who needs you, Tommy. So I won't be alone."

"I won't do it!"

Greaty laughs. "Well, seeing as how the boat is sinking and a storm's coming, it doesn't look like you have much of a choice. Not unless you can walk on water!"

A wave lifts the boat high and water pours in, filling the cabin. And then something tugs on Greaty's line so hard that it pulls the rod right out of his hand. The rod disappears into the water.

"I think it's time," he says.

I scramble into the flooding cabin and find a life jacket. I put it on, as if it can really help me.

*If you were Tommy, what would you do?*

When I come out, the water gets calm, and I feel something scraping along the bottom of the boat—something huge.

I look up to the sky, wishing that I could sprout wings and fly away from the sea. Then something rises out of the water in front of us—a big, slimy black fin the size of a great sail, and beneath that fin, two humps on a creature's back—a creature larger than any whale could possibly be.

"Look at that!" shouts Greaty.

The fin crosses before us, towering over our heads, and then submerges, disappearing into the black depths.

It gets very quiet, much too quiet. Greaty puts his hand on my shoulder.

"Thank you," he whispers. "Thank you, Tommy, for coming with me."

Somewhere below, I hear a rush of water as something coming from very, very deep forces its way toward the surface, getting closer and closer. The water around us begins to bubble and churn.

"No!" I scream, and climb up to the edge of the sinking boat.

I never thought that I would leap into the ocean by choice, but that's exactly what I do. My feet leave the gouged old wood of the *Mariana*, and in a moment I am underwater.

The water is icy cold all around me, salty and rough. I break surface, and gasp for air. My life jacket is all that keeps me from sinking into this bottomless ocean pit. A wave washes me away from the boat.

Then I hear a roar and the cracking of wood. A great gush of water catches me in the eyes, making them sting. I turn back, and see it only for an instant. Something huge, black, and covered with ooze. It has sharp teeth and no eyes, and a black, forked tongue that has forced its way through the hull of the boat, searching for Greaty like a tentacle . . . and finding him. The thing crushes the entire boat in its immense jaws. Its roar is so loud, I cannot hear if Greaty is screaming.

A wave hits, and I am under the water again. When I break surface, the beast, the boat, and Greaty are gone. Only churning water and bubbles remain where they had been.

Far away, I can see the dolphins waiting at the edge of this unholy water. I move my arms and kick my legs.

*I will not join you in your bottomless grave, Greaty. I will not let you take me with you. You will be alone. And even though I am out in the middle of the ocean at the edge of a storm, I will not die this way. I will not.*

Something huge and smooth brushes past my feet, but I don't think about it. Something rough and hard scrapes against my leg, but I only look forward, staring at the dolphins lined up a hundred yards away. Those dolphins are waiting for me, I know. They will not dare come into these waters, but if I make it back to them, I know that I will be all right. They will carry me home.

And so I will ignore the horrors that swarm unseen beneath me. I will close my ears to the roars and groans from the awful deep. And I will get to the dolphins, even if I have to walk on water.

**PREDICT**

*Will Tommy make it? What details make you think as you do?*

# RESTING DEEP

## ▼ Learning from the Story

The author of "Resting Deep" uses many similes—phrases that use the words *like* or *as* to compare two very unlike things. For example, on page 95, Tommy says he's "skinny as a rail."

Working with a partner, try to list all the similes in this story. See if you can find more similes than anyone else in class. Which of the author's comparisons is your favorite?

## ▼ Putting It into Practice

Try a word-association game to inspire some unique descriptions for your disastrous travel story. Work with a group of two or three classmates.

1. Write the name of a specific character or setting in your story on the board.
2. Ask the members of your group to say the first thing that comes to mind. List their responses under the character's name or the setting.
3. Write at least two similes using these word associations.

You must know
by now that SOS
doesn't stand
for Shipful Of
Sunshine!

Gina's father pointed to a yacht nestled in a <u>slip</u> at the end of the dock. "That's the one," he said. "Home sweet home for the next four weeks."

Gina let go of her mom's hand and ran down the length of the wooden dock for her first look at the boat her father had rented for their vacation. He had just finished some big project that had kept him so occupied for the last seven months that Gina's mom had begun making jokes about being a single mother. Finally he had finished, and to celebrate, he had rented this yacht from one of his clients.

Carefully Gina inspected the outside of the boat. If she was going to spend four weeks on this thing, she wanted to be sure there were no cracks or holes in it.

The yacht was just over forty feet long and had two <u>masts</u>—one in the front and one at the back. It was painted a blinding white, and it had polished wooden handrails along both sides of its deck. Along the back, Gina read the boat's name, *Penny Dreadful*.

"Well?" asked her mother as they caught up to her. "Is everything all right?"

**slip:** a parking-type space for boats at a dock

**masts:** long poles that hold the sails

**104** Lesson 9

"What does *Penny Dreadful* mean?" Gina asked, pointing to the name written on the back of the boat.

Her father laughed. "The woman who owns this yacht writes books. *Penny dreadful* is what they used to call a cheap, action-packed paperback."

"Odd name for a boat," Gina commented. "Well, it looks OK from the outside. What's it like inside?"

"There's only one way to find out," her dad said, pointing to the doorway that led into the cabin.

The cabin was much nicer than Gina had expected it to be. There was a large area that was a combination living room and kitchen. It was filled with every appliance she could think of, and all of them gleamed like new. The kitchen counters, made of rich, dark wood, were spotless as well, and the carpeting in the cabin was soft and clean. Continuing forward, Gina found two bedrooms—the first, a larger room with a double bed, and beyond that a small one up in the front of the hull. All of the furniture was modern, and the beds seemed comfortable. Gina nodded approvingly and went topside to give her dad her OK. Then she helped her parents unload the food and supplies they had packed for the trip.

Finally it was time to shove off, and Gina could hardly contain her excitement as her father untied the ropes that held them to the dock. Then, with one strong push from her father, the sailboat floated out into the calm waters of the <u>marina</u>. With Gina and her parents shouting orders and pretending they were pirates setting out to loot and plunder, the three glided smoothly out to sea.

Gina quickly grew accustomed to life on a boat. She had been afraid she would be seasick, but to her delight

marina: a place where pleasure-boat owners can dock their boats, have repairs done, and buy supplies

she found that the constant motion didn't bother her at all. When she mentioned this to her father, he laughed and pointed out that they were in pretty calm waters. Still, Gina felt that she could withstand whatever the ocean was going to throw at her.

Her parents' plan was to sail leisurely among the islands that dotted the waters in this part of the world. They had no specific goal in mind and were free to stay as long as they wanted on any particular island.

The first landing they made was on a small mountain poking up above the blue water. It was covered with lush tropical growth that looked like green velvet from a distance. As they drew closer, however, Gina could see long curves of shining white sand just waiting for her to lay a towel on. After her father had dropped anchor in a small bay, he rowed Gina and her mother to shore where they all sunbathed for a few hours.

But as it turned out, the island was deserted, and the family got bored. They decided to spend only a day there, lazing in the sun and exploring the dense jungle.

For Gina, the vacation became a series of minor variations on that first island stopover, except some of the islands had people living on them. If it wasn't for a friendly man on another yacht docked next to them on one of the populated islands, Gina would have really gotten tired of the same old routine. But the man was fascinating and full of real-life pirate tales that held her captivated for hours.

The man's name was Craig, and Gina's dad had <u>moored</u> next to his boat in the tiny marina that served the

**moored**: tied to a dock or held in place with an anchor

*What clues of upcoming disaster has the author planted so far?*

local islanders. With his brown, leathery skin marked with millions of tiny wrinkles, Gina thought Craig looked as if he'd spent his entire life baking under the sun.

He confirmed Gina's suspicions when he answered a question her father had asked. "Ayup, I've been sailing these waters for well on forty-five years, now."

"Forty-five years," Gina repeated in wonder. "Wow! You must have seen every inch of every island . . . everywhere."

Craig shrugged. "Seen a lot of 'em, I guess."

"We're on a casual tour," said Gina's father. "Any advice you can give us?"

---

**"Forty-five years," Gina repeated**

**in wonder. "Wow! You must**

**have seen every inch of every**

**island . . . everywhere."**

---

The old sailor thought for a moment, then nodded. "Ayup. Things are a little rough yonder round Leeward Isles. There's been a gang of pirates that's been causing a lot of trouble out there."

"Pirates?" Gina's mom asked doubtfully. "In this day and age?"

"Aye," Craig answered firmly. "Some things never change, except the boats they sail and the weapons they use."

"Is it dangerous?" asked Gina's dad.

grisly: horrible;
gruesome

**PREDICT**

*Notice how the author is starting to build suspense. Why do you think he mentions this particular legend?*

"Can be. But if you stay well away from the Leewards, you shouldn't have any problem. You have maps, right?"

When Gina's dad answered that they did, Craig clambered over and offered to point out the areas he'd been talking about. He disappeared below deck with Gina's dad, and the two men were gone for over an hour.

"I sure hope Craig will show my dad some exciting places to explore," Gina mumbled under her breath. "I'm tired of wandering around from island to island and sunbathing all day."

Gina and her parents spent two days on the small island, poking around the shops and taking bike rides through the interior. Gina was glad they weren't leaving right away. She was fascinated by their neighbor, Craig, and spent a lot of time listening to his collection of incredible stories. Pirates, old and new; fantastic creatures; glorious sea battles; mysterious ghost ships—the old man never seemed to run out of tales to tell.

Gina's favorite was the legend of the lost ship *Azrael*. According to Craig, the *Azrael* was the ghost of an old slave ship that had been carrying a full cargo of children when a fierce storm blew in. The captain, greedy to get his cargo of children to port so he could sell them, tried to sail through the storm even as it grew into a tremendous hurricane. The ship sank with all hands on deck, drowning the children who were still chained below.

"And ever since then," Craig said in a low voice, "the *Azrael* has sailed these waters, trying to make it to port. And the captain, even greedier in death, is said to be still searching for more children to add to his <u>grisly</u> cargo."

Gina shuddered in appreciation. Then, when Craig returned to his chores, she scampered off to write down as much of the story as she could remember. She wanted to tell it to her friends back home.

When they left the island, Gina's dad made sure to steer them away from the Leeward Isles. Instead, he pointed the *Penny Dreadful* toward a distant cluster of dots on the map, labeled the Hundred Atolls.

"I'm relatively sure we won't run into pirates there," he said, adding with a grin, "if there really are any."

But when they were a little less than two days away from the Hundred Atolls, something odd began to happen. They noticed a small speck—probably a boat—on the horizon behind them . . . and it appeared to be following them.

"Maybe it's one of the other boats we met?" Gina wondered out loud when she pointed out the distant vessel.

"We'll know for sure in a couple of days," her father said. "The Atolls are the only islands in this direction. We'll probably see them there."

But by the end of that day, Gina wasn't sure what the other ship was up to. As the setting sun turned the sky and sea into competing shades of gold, it was plain that the other ship had drawn closer as if it was, well, *chasing* after them. Now, instead of a formless black speck, Gina could just make out the billowing white sails of a very large ship.

Gina saw her parents having an animated discussion, but when they saw that she was watching, they ducked below into the <u>galley</u>. Not wasting another moment, Gina crept closer to hear what they were talking about.

**galley:** the kitchen on a boat

"I know," her father was saying, "but the simple fact that they're gaining on us means they must be moving under power."

"But that could be for any number of reasons," her mother answered. "It doesn't mean they're pirates."

"True. But after all those stories Craig was telling us, I'm just a little suspicious of any boat that has its sails up *and* its motor running. Especially when it's coming our way!"

Gina held her breath and strained to hear. *Pirates!* she thought, feeling electric tingles that were part fear, part excitement running through her.

"Look," her father continued, "all I'm saying is that it doesn't hurt us to lose a night's sleep. We'll put up full sail and keep an eye on the ship. That should put us comfortably ahead of it. Or, at the very least, keep us even."

"All right," her mother agreed. "That makes sense." Then she gave a small chuckle. "Looks like we won't be saving that coffee for the return trip."

True to her father's plan, they put up all the sails they had, causing the yacht to fairly leap across the tops of the waves. Gina kept her parents company as long as she could, but eventually made her way to her bunk. She had tried to ask them a few questions about what was going on, but had only gotten clipped, vague answers. *Anyway,* she thought as she dozed off, *at least down below I don't have to look at their tense faces.*

*If you were Gina, would you be able to sleep? Why or why not?*

The next morning Gina was up with the sun, and an ominous sight greeted her when she went on deck. Her mom and dad were sitting at the <u>tiller</u>, sipping mugs of coffee. They both looked more grim than they had the night before, and Gina could easily see why.

The ship behind them had drawn even closer in the night. Now it was easy to see that it was a gigantic sailing ship, much larger than the tiny yacht she was on. Its enormous sails were pulling away from its masts and looked like thick, billowing clouds hovering over the water. Gina, unable to see the bright gleam of paint in the sunlight, wondered if the ship behind them was hidden in the shadow of its sails or if it was painted some dark color.

"Is it really pirates?" Gina asked her parents after staring at the pursuing ship.

"I don't know," her father answered. "Whoever they are, they're in quite a hurry."

"Maybe we should start our engine," Gina's mother suggested quietly.

With one last glance at the pursuing ship, Gina's father nodded and went below, and after a few moments the powerful engines coughed into life with a reassuring rumble that gently vibrated the wooden deck. Instantly their yacht surged forward and began pulling away from the mysterious ship that trailed them.

The morning passed in tense silence. It seemed to Gina that the ship behind them had taken over her parents' thoughts. They absently replied to anything she said, and their eyes kept returning to the black ship behind them. It was her parents' obvious worry that frightened Gina the most, and her mind conjured up terrifying

tiller: a handle used to turn the rudder that steers a boat

pictures of horrible men swarming over the yacht and murdering her parents right in front of her eyes.

But even going as fast as they could, as the day lengthened, the distance between the two ships grew shorter.

"How can they be moving so fast?" Gina's father snapped to no one in particular. Muttering curses, he stomped down below to try and squeeze more power out of their own tiny engine. Gina's mother, looking extremely tense, went down with him, and Gina could hear the two of them whispering in frightened voices.

The ship was close enough now for Gina to see that it was a huge wooden vessel—at least three times the length of their yacht—with five separate sails that she could see. The middle part of the ship was lower than its front and back, and the whole craft was built of dark wood.

As Gina looked at the huge billowing sails, something about them seemed strange to her, but she couldn't figure out what. She then turned her eyes to the deck, where she could barely make out figures moving slowly about. That meant that they probably could see Gina and her parents, but for some reason they made no sign of greeting or of recognition. Gina shivered slightly. Obviously the people who were on board were not friendly fellow-travelers.

It was Gina's father who later pointed out the problem that had subconsciously bothered her. "Those sails sure are odd," he mumbled, staring at the pursuing ship. Then suddenly he opened his eyes wide in surprise and pointed at the dark vessel. "That's impossible!" he gasped.

"What?" Gina asked, peering at the black ship.

"The sails . . ." He groped for words. "The sails . . . they're pointing the wrong way!"

Suddenly Gina understood. She looked up at the sails of their own boat. The wind was pushing from the left, blowing the sails out and over the other side of the boat. But the sails of the black ship stood straight out from the masts, as if the wind was coming from directly behind.

Even Gina, with her short experience sailing, knew this was impossible. And her heart seemed to freeze to a halt as a horrible thought exploded in her mind. *The Azrael*, she thought in terror. *It's coming for me!*

---

**"What?" Gina asked, peering at the black ship.**

**"The sails . . ." He groped for words.**

**"The sails . . . they're pointing the wrong way!"**

---

She turned to her father, fear stretching her face into a mask of wide eyes and a gaping mouth. "We've got to go faster, Dad," she urged. "Craig told me about that ship—it's a ghost ship looking for children to sell as slaves!"

Gina's father looked at her strangely, and she could tell he thought she was so scared she was talking crazy. He rested a hand on her head. "We'll be OK," he

*Compare the description of this ship with the description of Gina's yacht.*

**leprous:** scaly

**resistance:** opposing force

promised. "We should have the first of the Atolls in sight by late this afternoon, and I don't think whoever's on that ship will try anything when we're that close to land."

"Please go faster," Gina urged.

Seeing his daughter's tremendous fear, her father nodded and went back below to talk things over with her mother.

Gina glanced back at the horrible ship. She watched in amazement and terror as the terrible black ship drew closer. It was as if her thoughts had given it renewed power!

Now, the sails looked tattered and <u>leprous</u> and seemed to glow with pale bolts of lightning that flickered around the masts. The dark wood of the hull revealed itself to be black with slime, like something from the bottom of the sea. And the huge bow made no wave as it pushed closer. It was as if the ancient wood offered no <u>resistance</u> to the blue-green water—as if it didn't sail on the sea, but floated above it.

Gina heard a gasp of sharply drawn breath at her side and turned to see her mother standing with one hand to her mouth. "Mom," Gina sobbed, pointing to the ghost ship, "we've got to get out of here! Can't we go any faster?"

Without answering, her mother turned and went back down to the engines.

Gina remained at the rail, hypnotized by the thing that was chasing them. In horror, she watched the figures of the crew, staring at their ragged clothing, torn so badly that it showed glimpses of their skin, pale as a fish belly. And all of the disgusting figures had a terribly bloated, diseased appearance, too, as they snapped to the attention of a grinning skeleton that stood at the highest deck of the ship, with its bony arms folded across its chest.

But even worse was the huddled group of children standing at the front of the ship. Although dressed in many different styles of clothing, they all had in common a heavy iron chain running from one neck collar to the next, connecting them in a long line.

"No," Gina mumbled. "Not me. I'm not going to be one of them."

Then an explosion slammed her to the deck. Black smoke poured out of the open hatch that led below deck.

"They're attacking!" Gina screamed as the yacht lurched to one side, then began tilting slowly backward.

She fought her way up the slanting deck to peer through the oily smoke into the <u>salon</u> where her parents had been. Water was bubbling up from below, and the room was already filling with water. Horrified, Gina saw her mother floating facedown in the dirty seawater. "Mom!" she screamed, then looked frantically for her father, who was nowhere to be seen.

"No!" Gina screamed, throwing herself into the water to her mother's side. She rolled the body over and saw clearly that her mother was no longer alive. Then, bursting into tears, Gina starting yelling for her father like a madwoman.

Suddenly the yacht lurched, throwing the dead body of her father overboard. Gina screamed as the boat settled farther into the water. Now the salt water was beginning to wash over the deck railings, and Gina saw faint streams begin to trickle down the steps from above. Choking on

salon: a large room, like a living room

her tears, she waded to the steps and climbed onto the deck. Then, looking back for just a second, she flung herself into the water as the yacht, along with the bodies of her parents, sank.

As she paddled around in circles, crying and trying to keep her head above water, Gina suddenly felt an icy breeze wash over her wet back. Looking up through bleary eyes, she saw the black, slime-coated hull of the *Azrael* beside her. Two <u>animate</u> corpses were hanging from some ropes, and their decaying arms were stretched toward her. Far above them were dozens of children, their dead eyes staring down at Gina.

"No!" she screamed, then burst into furious kicking. But as hard as she tried, Gina couldn't seem to move her body. And soon, cold hands grasped her arms and began hauling her up.

"Please!" Gina pleaded as she tried to struggle. "Don't take me with you!"

But then, one of the children turned her empty eye sockets on Gina and pointed at something below her in the water. Retching with fear, Gina turned to see the body of a small girl—*her* body—sinking slowly beneath the waves.

**animate:** moving as if alive

# THE FLYING DUTCHMAN

Three quarters of the earth is covered by water. The great oceans are the keepers of mysteries and the <u>spawning</u> grounds of myths—stories of sea monsters, mermaids, and the like. Perhaps the most horrifying is the tale of the *Flying Dutchman*.

According to the legend, a 17th-century Dutch sea captain, Cornelius Vanderdecken, was known for taking extreme risks even in stormy seas. On a disastrous trip around the Cape of Good Hope at the southern tip of Africa, during a fierce storm, he chose a short but dangerous route close to the rocky shore. When one terrified sailor begged him to change his mind, the captain threw the unfortunate man overboard. Vanderdecken then defiantly shook his fist at the heavens and swore that he would sail his ship until Judgment Day, if necessary. Suddenly, a glowing figure appeared on the deck and declared that Vanderdecken had chosen his own fate. The ship was condemned to sail forever without reaching port. To this day, some sailors believe that the ship, which has come to be known as the *Flying Dutchman*, still sails, and that its sighting is a warning of <u>impending</u> doom.

**Sightings of ghost ships—real or imagined—always build suspense!**

**spawning:** beginning

**impending:** about to happen

**True to the legend, on the day of the sighting, the man who had first seen the *Flying Dutchman* was killed in a fall from the fore topmast.**

Is this just one more fanciful tale of the sea? Strangely, sightings of the arrogant sea captain and his cursed vessel have been reported for 300 years. It is probably accurate to chalk up most of the sightings to a trick of light or perhaps an overly tired sailor with an active imagination, but some reports are not so easily dismissed. In 1881, one frightening account was sworn to by 13 sailors (including the captain) of the HMS *Bacchante*. The night was clear and the sea was calm. In the log, the captain of the *Bacchante* described the ghost ship as passing silently across the bow, bathed in an eerie red glow. The ancient masts and rigging were unmistakable. One of the witnesses, a young midshipman, is considered a particularly reliable source. He would eventually be known as George V, the king of England.

True to the legend, on the day of the sighting, the man who had first seen the *Flying Dutchman* was killed in a fall from the fore topmast. Tragedy also awaited the captain of the *Bacchante*. When he finally reached port, he felt the need to see a doctor and was given the news that he was dying of a fatal illness.

The phantom ship evidently has been seen many times since, but one sighting was especially interesting because it included a phantom storm. In 1911, the whaling ship *Orkney Belle* was off the coast of Iceland in fairly calm seas when the crew reportedly witnessed the *Flying Dutchman* battling a nonexistent storm. The ghost ship rose and fell in the waves, and its sails strained in the wind as it raced by the *Orkney Belle*, but the terrified sailors felt no signs of a real storm. Fortunately, unlike the crew of the *Bacchante*, none of the whaler's crew suffered any harm.

## ▼ Learning from the Story

See if you can figure out how the author builds suspense in "SOS." With a small group, take turns reading the first few pages of the story. What tone did you use when you read? Did you feel like you were telling a cheery travel story or a tale of horror?

Now take turns reading paragraphs from the end of the story. Did your tone of voice change when you read those pages? Did you read faster? Did you feel more tension? What techniques did the author use to build suspense? List the techniques. Share your list with the class.

## ▼ Putting It into Practice

Look over your own disastrous travel story. Were you successful at building suspense? Your readers should spend far more time anticipating the horror than they spend actually experiencing it. Try the following techniques to build suspense.

- Make your sentences get shorter gradually.
- Use easier and easier (shorter and simpler) words.
- Sprinkle in more and more words that hint at death and horror. Paint darker pictures in your readers' minds.

# ConnectingFlight

Some people look forward to a **trip**. Others think of it as a **disaster** just waiting to happen. Can you guess which kind of person **Jana is?**

The narrow, doorless hall seems to stretch on forever. The bag slung across her shoulder seems full of lead.

And the image of her parents waving good-bye still sticks in her mind.

With a boarding pass in hand, Jana Martinez walks down a narrow, tilted corridor, toward the 737 at the end of the Jetway.

She tries to forget the strange state of cold <u>limbo</u> that fills the gap between her parents behind her and her final destination—Wendingham Prep School.

It is only three hours away now—just a two-hour flight from Chicago to Boston, and then an hour's bus ride. Still, to Jana, this empty time between two places always seems to last an eternity.

She reaches the door of the plane, stumbling over the lip of the hatch, and a flight attendant grabs her arm too tightly. "Watch your step," the flight attendant says, trying to help Jana keep her balance.

**limbo:** a place for forgotten people; a place lost between two locations

**PREDICT**

*Is there anything significant about the flight attendant's warning? How might this be a sign of things to come?*

Now, as she makes her way down the narrow aisle, Jana wonders if the flight attendant's overly strong grip will leave a bruise on her arm. She is sure the cruel strap of her carry-on bag will leave her black and blue.

The plane is divided by a single center aisle, and each row has three seats on either side. Jana finds her seat by the window on the left side of the plane. She has to climb over a heavy, pale woman to get there, and just as she finally settles in, her sense of loneliness settles in deeper than before.

*I'm surrounded by strangers,* she thinks. *I'm unknown to all of them . . . and unconnected.*

The plane is filled with people she's never seen before and will never see again—filled with hundreds of lives that intersect nowhere but on this plane. The feeling is eerie to Jana, and unnatural.

The woman beside her is several sizes too large for the seat, and her large body spreads toward Jana, taking over Jana's armrest, and forcing her to lean uncomfortably against the cold window.

"Sorry, dearie," says the woman, with a British accent. "You'd think people have no hips, the way they build these seats."

The woman also has bad breath.

Jana sighs, calculates how many seconds there are in a two-hour flight, and begins to count down from seven-thousand-two-hundred. She wonders if a flight could possibly be any worse. Soon she finds out that it can.

A woman with a baby takes the seat next to the large English woman, and the moment the plane leaves the ground, the baby begins an ear-splitting screech-fest. The mother tries to console the child, but it does no good. Grimacing, Jana notices a man sitting across the aisle turn down his hearing aid.

"Why do I always end up on Screaming Baby Airlines?" Jana grumbles to herself, and the large woman in her airspace accidentally overhears. She turns to Jana with a smile.

"It's the pressure in its ears, the poor thing," says the large woman, pointing to the wailing baby. Then she adds something curious. "Babies on planes comfort me, actually. I always think, God won't crash a plane carrying a baby."

The thought that seems to give so much comfort to the large woman only gives Jana the creeps. She peers out her window, watching as the plane rises above little puffs of clouds that soon look like tiny white specks far below.

"We've reached our cruising altitude of 35,000 feet, and *blah, blah, blah*," drones the captain, who seems to have the same voice as every other airline pilot in the world. It's as if they go to some special school that teaches them all how to sound exactly alike.

The baby, having exhausted its screaming machine, can only whimper now, and the plump woman, who has introduced herself as Moira Lester, turns to Jana and asks, "You'll be visiting someone in Boston, then?"

"School," says Jana curtly, not feeling like having a conversation with a stranger.

"Boarding school, is it?" asks Moira, not taking the hint. "I went to boarding school. It's all the <u>rage</u> back in Britain. Not many of them in the States, are there?" And then she begins to spin the never-ending tale of her

**rage:** the fashion; a fad

uninteresting family, all the boarding schools they attended, why they went there, and which classmates have become famous people that Jana has never heard of.

Jana nods as if listening but tries to tune her out by gazing out the window at the specks of clouds below. It is just about then that the feeling comes. It's a sensation—a twinge, like a spark of static electricity darting through her, that causes a tiny, tiny change in air pressure. It's like a pinprick in her reality—a feeling so slight that it takes a while for Jana to realize that she has felt anything at all.

As she turns from the window to look around her, nothing appears to have changed: Moira is still talking, the baby is still whimpering.

But as for Jana, she has a clear sense that something is suddenly not right.

"Something wrong, dearie?" Moira asks.

But Jana just shakes her head, trying to convince herself that it's only her imagination.

Then, about ten minutes later, Jana asks, "Where's the old man?" The sense of something wrong had been growing and growing within her, and now, she has finally noticed something different.

The mother, bouncing her baby on her knee, looks at Jana oddly. "What old man?" she asks.

"You know—the man who was sitting across the aisle from you. He was wearing a hearing aid."

The mother turns to look. Sitting across the aisle is a businessman with slick black hair. Certainly not old, and definitely not wearing a hearing aid, he sits reading a magazine in seat 16-D as if he belongs there.

**PREDICT**

*What could have happened to the man with the hearing aid?*

"Don't you remember him?" Jana persists. "He turned down his hearing aid when your baby was screaming."

The mother shrugs. "I didn't notice," she says. "Who notices anybody on airplanes these days?"

"Looks like there are some empty seats on the plane," suggests Moira. "Perhaps this man you're talking about moved."

Jana sighs. "Yeah, maybe that's it," she <u>concedes</u>, although not really convinced. She would have noticed if the man had gotten up.

"Excuse me," Jana says and climbs over Moira and the mother and her baby, then heads down the aisle to the bathroom. There is something wrong, she knows it. Something terribly wrong. She can feel it in the pit of her stomach, like the feeling you get a few minutes before becoming violently ill.

Jana pushes her way through the narrow bathroom doorway and into the tight little compartment. Jana looks in the mirror, then splashes cold water on her face. *Maybe it's just the excitement of going back to school,* she tells herself. *Maybe it's just airsickness.*

But where is that man with the hearing aid?

She dries her face with a paper towel and makes her way back to her seat, looking in every row for the old man. She goes to the very front of the plane. No old man with a hearing aid. What did he do? Jump off the plane?

When Jana returns to her seat, the mother and baby have moved to where she can lay her baby down on an empty seat—a few rows back on the other side of the plane. As Jana looks around, she notices that there are

concedes: agrees, with hesitation

empty seats, and even empty rows on the plane now—but all the vacant seats appear to be on the side of the plane opposite her.

Jana stands there watching as several people from her side of the plane shift over to make use of the empty rows, making more room for everyone. How odd—the plane seemed crowded when she got on.

When Jana retakes her seat, Moira welcomes her back with a wide, friendly smile. Jana forces her own smile, and as she settles in, she happens to glance out the window . . . then freezes.

"Moira," she says, "everything's covered in clouds!"

Moira glances out the window at the cotton-thick clouds rolling toward the horizon below. "Why, I suppose it is," she says.

"Excuse me," Jana says as she climbs back over Moira and crosses the aisle. She then leans awkwardly over the businessman and two other passengers to get a look out their window. She is certain she hadn't seen clouds out of the other side of the plane on her way back from the bathroom.

Sure enough, from this window, Jana can see the ground—a patchwork quilt of greens and browns gilded by the afternoon sun.

"It—it's *different* on this side of the plane," she observes, her voice shaky.

"So what?" asks the businessman, annoyed at the way Jana is still leaning across him. "We must be traveling along the edge of a front. You know—the line where cold air meets warm air, and storm clouds form."

Jana just stares at him, feeling her hands growing colder by the moment. *It's a logical explanation,* she thinks, *but it's wrong.*

Quietly Jana returns to her seat. She pulls out the magazine in the pouch in front of her and tries to read it, but finds nothing can take her attention away from the clouds beneath her window, and the perfectly clear sky on the other side of the plane.

That's when the captain comes on the loudspeaker again.

"Just thought I'd let you know," he says in his every-pilot voice, "that we'll be passing Mount Rushmore shortly. If you look out the right side of the plane, you'll be able to see it on the horizon."

Jana doesn't bother to look, since she's on the left side. But she does notice that people on her side of the plane are chuckling, as if the pilot has made some kind of joke.

Then it hits her.

Geography was never one of Jana's best subjects, but she's sure that Mount Rushmore is not in Ohio—the state they should have been over right now! She turns to Moira. "Where is Mount Rushmore?" she asks, trying not to sound panicked.

"Can't say for sure," the heavyset woman replies. "I haven't been in the States long."

"This *is* the flight to Boston, isn't it?"

"As far as I know," says Moira. "At least that's what my ticket says."

Jana uneasily mulls over everything as she goes back to staring out her window . . . at nothing but clouds.

Why does Jana think this explanation is wrong?

About an hour and a half into the flight, Jana has bitten her nails down to stubs—a habit she thought she had broken years ago. That tiny tear in the fabric of her safe and sane world that happened a while back has widened so rapidly, Jana wonders if it can ever be sewn back together again.

It is now dark outside her window. Jana reasons that that is perfectly normal. She has flown enough to know that when flying east at dusk, the sun always sets behind you incredibly fast. It has to do with the curvature of the earth, and time zones, and that sort of thing. Perfectly natural . . . except that the sun is still shining on the other side of the plane.

The plane is filled with anxious murmurs. Perhaps Jana was the first one to realize things were screwy, but now everyone sees it.

"There's some explanation," one person whispers.

"We'll probably all laugh about it later," another says.

And indeed, some people are laughing already, as if laughing could make it all better.

Sitting there, with no nails left to bite, Jana wonders if it is always like this when things go wrong in midair. Do people not scream and wail the way they do in the movies? Do they get quiet . . . like this . . . or just whisper, or laugh? And if they do scream, do they only scream on the inside?

Jana calls the flight attendant over.

"Excuse me," she says, her voice quivering with panic, "but we have to land this plane. We have to land it *now!*"

The flight attendant smiles and speaks with practiced

**PREDICT**

*What do you think happened to the plane?*

reassurance, as if Jana is nothing more than an anxious flier. "We've begun our final descent," she tells her. "We should be on the ground shortly."

"Haven't you looked out the window?" Jana snaps at the flight attendant. "Haven't you seen what's happening out there?"

"Weather conditions up here," says the flight attendant, "aren't like weather conditions on the ground."

"Night and day aren't weather conditions!" shouts Jana. The nervous murmurs can now be heard around the cabin.

The flight attendant looks into Jana's eyes, grits her teeth furiously, and says, "I'll have to ask you to sit down, miss."

That look on the flight attendant's face says everything. It says, *We have no idea what's going on, but we can't admit that, you stupid girl! If we do, everyone will start panicking. So shut your face before we shut it for you!*

The flight attendant storms away, and Jana dares to do something she's been wanting to do since the sky began to change. She looks across the aisle to the businessman and asks him where he's going.

"Seattle," he says. "I'm going to Seattle—of course—just like you."

Several people on Jana's side of the plane gasp and whisper to one another, as if being quiet about it makes the situation any less horrific than it is.

"I thought this flight was going to Boston," says Moira.

"She's right," says another passenger behind Moira. "This plane is going to Boston."

The businessman swallows. "There must be some sort

of . . . computer mix-up."

Jana sinks in her seat as the plane passes through the heavy cloud cover—on *her* side of the plane—and as soon as they punch through the clouds, she can see the twinkling lights of a city below. She doesn't dare look out the windows on the other side of the plane anymore.

*In Seattle,* Jana thinks, *it would still be light out.*

The truth was simple, and at the same time impossible to comprehend. Somehow, some grand computer glitch—not in any simple airline computer—got two flights . . . confused.

*A flight like this will never reach the ground,* she tells herself. *How can it?*

Suddenly the plane shudders and whines as the landing gear doors open. People are all looking out their windows at the night on the left side of the plane, and then at the day on the right. Slowly cold terror paints their faces a pale white.

Across the aisle and three rows back, the baby screams again as they descend. To Jana, the screams are far less disturbing than the whispers and silences of all the other passengers, but not to everyone.

"Shut that child up!" shouts the businessman.

But the mother can do nothing but hold her baby close to her as they sit across the narrow aisle, waiting for the plane to touch down.

*Across the aisle?* Jana's mind suddenly screams. And then that sickening feeling that began almost two hours ago spreads through her arms and legs, until every part of her body feels weak. Jana glances at the empty seat right next

to Moira and erupts with panic. She opens her seat belt, stands and shouts to the mother, yelling louder than the woman's screaming baby.

"Get up!" Jana shouts. "You have to come back to this seat!"

"But we're landing," says the mother nervously. "I shouldn't unbuckle my seat belt."

"You're not *supposed* to be there!" Jana insists. "You started on *this* side. I can't explain it now—but you have to come back to this side of the plane—NOW!"

*Why does Jana insist that the mother return to her side of the plane?*

Terrified, the mother unbuckles her seat belt and, clutching her screaming baby, crosses the aisle the moment the tires touch the runway. Others who had moved to the empty seats on the right side sense what is about to happen. They race to get out of their seat belts and back to their original seats—but they are not fast enough.

In an instant, there is a burst of flame, and the world seems to end.

"Help me!" screams the mother.

Jana grabs the woman's hand, while Moira grabs the baby. They fall into the seat next to Moira, and the mother shields her baby from the nightmare exploding around them.

Everyone screams as the plane spins and tumbles out of control—everyone but Jana. She glances out her window to see that nothing seems wrong. The plane is landing in Boston, just like planes always land.

But on the other side of the plane, the *right* side of the plane, there is smoke and flames and shredding steel. And, beyond the shattering windows, the ground is rolling over and over. In awe, Jana watches as the smoke billows . . .

but *stays* on the other side of the aisle. In fact, Jana can't even smell it!

Moira leans into Jana. "Don't look!" she cries. "You mustn't look at it!"

And Jana knows that Moira is right. So instead, she holds Moira's hand and turns to look out her own window. Tears rolling down her cheeks, she watches the terminal roll peacefully toward her. She feels the plane calmly slow down, and she tries to ignore the awful wails from the other side of the plane . . . until the last wail trails off.

Then the captain begins to speak, uncertain at first, but then with building confidence. "Uh . . . on behalf of our crew, I'd like to welcome you to . . . Boston. Please remain seated until we are secure at the terminal."

The screaming has stopped. The only sound now is that of the engines powering down to a low whine. Slowly Jana dares to look across the aisle.

There, she finds the man with the hearing aid staring back at her, <u>aghast</u>.

On the other side of the plane are all the people who had been there when they had taken off. Now that Jana sees their faces, she can recognize them.

*Someone must have fixed the computer,* Jana thinks, and then she turns to Moira. "Do you suppose that while we were watching the right half of that flight to Seattle—"

"—that the people on the other side were watching the left half?" finishes Moira. "Look at their faces. I can only imagine that they were."

The mother, whose baby has stopped screaming and

aghast: frightened

has fallen asleep, thanks Jana with tears in her eyes. Jana touches the baby's fine hair, then smiles. Suddenly it seems that all those long stories Moira has told on the plane don't seem so boring, and in a way Jana longs to hear all of them again. In fact, she longs to hear every story of every person on that plane. *There are so many lives intersecting on an airplane,* she thinks. *So many stories to hear!*

Jana walks with Moira to the baggage claim, where suitcases are already flying down the <u>chute</u> and circling on the baggage carousel. There, Jana watches people from her flight greet friends and family who have been waiting for them.

"I just heard that a flight out west didn't make it," someone says. "It was the same airline, too."

But no one from Jana's flight says anything. How can you tell someone that you saw a plane crash from the inside, but it wasn't *your* plane?

"It's good that things ended up back where they belong," Moira says.

"There's nothing 'good,' about it," says Jana flatly.

"No, I suppose not," Moira agrees. "But it's right. Right and proper."

Together, Jana and Moira wait a long time for their luggage, but it never comes. Jana has to admit that she didn't expect it to.

Not when all the luggage coming down the chute is ticketed to Seattle.

Notice the change in Jana's attitude—and in the author's tone.

chute: a tube for sliding things down

**Connecting*Flight***

### ▼ Learning from the Story

What have you learned about putting together a story? Do this activity with a group of classmates.

1. Fold a sheet of paper into three columns. Label the columns Characters, Setting, and Problem.

2. Under Characters, write the names of two story characters. Add some identifying characteristics— jobs, ages, something unique about their personalities. Fold that column to the inside and pass the sheet to the group to your right.

3. Do NOT look at the character descriptions! Under Setting, write a quick description of a setting for a story. Turn that column under and pass the sheet to the group to your right.

4. Do NOT look at the Characters or Setting! Under Problem, quickly write down a problem or predicament that a story could revolve around. Now pass your finished paper to the right.

Your group now has characters, a setting, and a problem. All you have to do is put these three elements together into a story! Take 15 minutes to write a first draft of a story. After everyone has finished, share your group's draft with the class.

## ▼ Putting It into Practice

Give your own travel tale of terror one final check. Ask yourself these questions.

- Is my story clear and easy to follow?
- Are major details and character and setting descriptions woven throughout the story?
- Have I used dialogue to tell the story, as well as to reveal information about my characters?
- Have I built up suspense so my readers will sit on the edges of their seats?

Now you're ready for the real test—having someone else read your story. Have a classmate read your story and give you feedback. What does your reader like about your story? What problems does he or she have with it? Can you use these comments to make your story clearer or better? Remember, it's not too late to revise your story one more time!